"Lucas...I know no a thousand times, but please, will you consider holding off on the sale of Rothwell Park until after Delphine's wedding?"

Lucas let out a long-winded sigh. "You don't let up, do you?"

"I've learned you don't achieve your goals in life unless you're prepared to work at them. My credo is 'If you've got what it takes, then do whatever it takes.'"

An enigmatic smile played at the edges of his mouth. Ruby sensed he was mulling something over in his mind. Making calculations that somehow involved her. It gave her a secret thrill to think he might be prepared to cut a deal with her. "All right, you can hold the wedding here. But I want something in return."

Ruby's heart did a jerky somersault. "We're prepared to negotiate on a hiring fee."

"I'm not talking about money."

She moistened her parchment-dry lips. "You're... you're not?"

"I want you to come with me to Greece."

Weddings Worth Billions

Say yes...to the wedding of your dreams!

At Happily Ever After Weddings, nothing short of perfection will do! Best friends Ruby, Harper and Aerin will not rest until they give each uber-rich client a wedding beyond their wildest dreams.

Still, while the trio witness true love on an almost daily basis, they have yet to experience it themselves. Will the arrival of three billionaires lead Ruby, Harper and Aerin to say "I do," too?

Discover more with...

Ruby and Lucas's story
Cinderella's Invitation to Greece
Available now!

Harper's and Aerin's stories
Coming soon!

Melanie Milburne

CINDERELLA'S INVITATION TO GREECE

ISBN-13: 978-1-335-56956-1

Cinderella's Invitation to Greece

Copyright © 2022 by Melanie Milburne

For questions and comments about the quality of this book, please contact us at CustomerService@Harlequin.com.

Harlequin Enterprises ULC
22 Adelaide St. West, 41st Floor
Toronto, Ontario M5H 4E3, Canada
www.Harlequin.com

Printed in U.S.A.

Melanie Milburne read her first Harlequin novel at the age of seventeen, in between studying for her final exams. After completing a master's degree in education, she decided to write a novel, and thus her career as a romance author was born. Melanie is an ambassador for the Australian Childhood Foundation and a keen dog lover and trainer. She enjoys long walks in the Tasmanian bush. In 2015 Melanie won the HOLT Medallion, a prestigious award honoring outstanding literary talent.

Books by Melanie Milburne

Harlequin Presents

The Billion-Dollar Bride Hunt

The Scandalous Campbell Sisters

Shy Innocent in the Spotlight
A Contract for His Runaway Bride

Once Upon a Temptation

His Innocent's Passionate Awakening

Wanted: A Billionaire

One Night on the Virgin's Terms
Breaking the Playboy's Rules
One Hot New York Night

Visit the Author Profile page
at Harlequin.com for more titles.

To Polly, my gorgeous miniature poodle who crossed the rainbow bridge recently. You were the most amazing dog—always submissive, always sweet and loving, a wonderful mother to Lily and adoring grandmother to the late Gonzo. And an especially fabulous granny to your human grandkids! I wrote ninety-plus books with you lying on your bed next to my desk.
You are greatly missed.

CHAPTER ONE

RUBY PENNINGTON DROVE up the long hedge-row-lined driveway of Rothwell Park with a flutter of moth wings in her belly. Coming 'home' to the grand Yorkshire moors estate always triggered a mixture of emotions. Never more so than when she knew Lucas Rothwell was in residence. And, as much as she longed to catch up with her grandmother over the long weekend, it was Lucas she really needed to see.

Thick, bruised-looking clouds scudded across the sky, with the sun appearing weakly between them again and again, as if still deciding whether to call it quits for the day. In the distance, rain was sweeping in from the moors in slanted grey sheets, and the wind was whistling and howling like a siren announcing impending doom.

Ruby brought her car to a stop near the old stables and turned off the engine.

Don't be nervous. Don't be nervous. Don't be nervous.

Her mentally chanted pep talk was falling seriously short. The moth wings in her belly had turned into bats. Hundreds of frantically flapping bats. It was impossible not to be a little jittery around Lucas Rothwell. How long had it been since she'd seen him face to face? Years. She never usually came home unless she knew he wasn't there.

But this time was different.

She *had* to see him.

As soon as Ruby got out of the car the biting wind whipped her hair around her face and needles of ice pricked her skin. Just as well the wild and capricious weather of the Yorkshire moors was exactly what her American celebrity client wanted for her wedding. It would be the highest profile wedding Ruby had done so far, and she owed it to her best friends and business partners, Harper and Aerin, to secure this venue. Their business, Happy Ever After Weddings, was making good progress, but this wedding would lift their profile way more than they could have dreamed possible when they'd first brainstormed a business plan on the back of a napkin in their favourite coffee shop.

Ruby brushed her hair away with her hand and walked towards the imposing front entrance of the castle. The centuries-old estate was a spectacular setting for a fairy tale wedding. The gothic-style castle with its multiple turrets and grandly appointed wings could house numerous guests, and the industrial-sized kitchen was perfect for catering for a crowd.

Pulling off this celebrity wedding gig would be her way of proving she had what it took to rise above her hardscrabble beginnings and being viewed as nothing more than the unwanted kid of a drug addict. Ruby didn't allow herself to think of failing once she set out to do something. Failure had been modelled to her by her mother, and Ruby was determined not to follow her example. Besides, her friends and business partners were relying on her.

And when people relied on her she delivered.

Before Ruby could put her key in the lock, the door opened a crack.

'Ruby, lass, what you are you doing here?' Her grandmother's shocked expression wasn't exactly the welcome Ruby was expecting. It had been months since she'd been to Rothwell Park. And, although her gran wasn't the overly effusive sort, surely she could summon up a teensy bit of enthusiasm?

'I told you weeks ago I'd be here for the Bank Holiday weekend.'

Her grandmother cast a furtive glance over her shoulder and then, keeping the front door only just ajar, whispered, 'Now's not a good time. The master's here and he doesn't want visitors.'

Ruby mentally rolled her eyes at her grandmother's old-fashioned habit of referring to Lucas Rothwell as 'the master'. Clearly her gran had been watching too many period dramas. And as for Lucas being in residence—that was the whole reason for Ruby's visit. Her gran had mentioned a few weeks ago about his planning to be in Yorkshire this weekend, after spending months flitting between Greece and Italy for work. Ruby wouldn't have travelled all this way from London if he wasn't going to be home.

'Why? Has he got one of his supermodel girlfriends here?'

It wouldn't be the first time Ruby had come across Lucas entertaining one of his glamorous partners. She had spent her childhood and adolescence pretending not to notice his brooding good looks and the way his lovers gazed up at him adoringly. She had pretended not to be jealous that he never looked at her the way he looked at those beautiful women. But then, as the homeless ten-year-old waif who had come to live with her housekeeper grandmother after the imprisonment of her mother, Ruby had been practically invisible to him.

Her grandmother pursed her lips, but still kept the door half closed. 'He's alone, but—'

'Great—because he's the one I really need to see.' Ruby smiled and, pushing the door open a little further, bent down to give her gran a smacking kiss on the cheek. 'Not that it isn't always lovely to see you,' she added.

'Get away with you, child.'

Her gran brushed Ruby away as if she was an annoying insect but there was no malice in it. After a rough upbringing herself, her gran had trouble showing and receiving affection, and even while Ruby had longed for more kisses and cuddles growing up, she didn't feel any less loved. Her gran had taken her in and raised her, and for that she would be for ever grateful. Rothwell Park had been the first stable home she had experienced. The castle and its grounds had provided her with security and shelter, which had been the complete opposite of the chaos of moving from one flea-infested bedsit to another while her mother tried to outrun her debts.

Ruby stepped past to enter the castle and her grandmother closed the door behind her with a soft click, her expression still troubled. 'I shouldn't have mentioned he'd be home this weekend.'

Her gran's stage whisper echoed eerily through the large entrance hall and made the fine hairs on the back of Ruby's neck stand up at the roots.

'He expressly told me to keep out all visitors.'

'I'm hardly a visitor.'

Her gran wrung her hands in an agitated manner, her eyes flicking towards the grand staircase as if she was expecting to see Lucas come striding down to fire her on the spot for disobeying his orders.

'You can't stay. He won't allow it.'

Ruby scrunched up her face in scorn. 'Oh, don't be so dramatic, Gran. Of course he'll allow it. This was my home for years.

Besides, I have important business to discuss with him. Where is he?'

Her gran's throat moved up and down over a convulsive swallow. 'The library. I was about to take his cup of tea up to him. But—'

'I'll do it for you.'

Why Lucas couldn't fetch his own cup of tea was not worth arguing about with her gran. Beatrice Pennington was an old-school housekeeper. The upstairs and downstairs divide had never been breached in the whole time Ruby had lived with her grandmother.

Lucas's parents, Claudia and Lionel, had occasionally invited her and her gran to join them for Christmas and other gatherings, but Beatrice had been adamant about keeping the distinction of employer and employee in place. Ruby had quietly and covertly rebelled by finding a hideout position, from which to observe the grand and often raucous dinner parties Claudia and Lionel had hosted. The Rothwells had lived in a completely different world from the one she had been born into. She'd been endlessly fascinated by their glamorous, exciting whirl of wealth and flamboyance and over-the-top decadence.

Ruby couldn't help noticing her gran wincing as she prepared the tea tray. 'Have you hurt your arm?' she asked. 'Here, let me look at you.'

'It's nothing.'

Ruby took the kettle out of her grandmother's hand and set it back on the bench. She turned her gran's wrist over and saw the angry red welt of a recent burn. The skin was raw and weeping, the edges a purply-red that hinted at a possible infection. 'Gran, that needs dressing. It looks like it's getting—'

Her grandmother pulled her wrist out of Ruby's hold. 'Stop fussing, lass. I've had worse in my time.'

'Maybe, but you're older now, and wound infections can turn nasty in a blink. You really should see a doctor. You might need a skin graft or something. I can take you after I've spoken to—'

'I don't need a doctor,' her gran said with a determined edge to her voice. 'Now, take that tea up to the master before it gets stone-cold.'

Ruby shook her head in frustration, and then glanced at the tea tray. 'Oh, yum, parkin. I haven't had that in months.' She reached for a second cup and plate, and placed them on the tray next to the others.

Her gran looked aghast. 'What are you doing?'

'I'm going to have afternoon tea with Lucas.'

'You'll have me fired, that's what.' Her gran's tone was gruff, but her expression was set in deep trench lines of worry.

Ruby scooped up the tray. 'You know, you really should think about retiring. This place is too big for you now, and you're not getting any younger.'

'I'll retire when I'm good and ready and not a moment before.'

Ruby knew better than to argue with her gran in one of her mulish moods. But that was another conversation she would have to have with Lucas Rothwell—about her gran's retirement.

'I'll help you with dinner after I've spoken to Lucas.'

The library was on the ground floor, several hundred metres from the kitchen, which only reinforced Ruby's concerns about her gran's increasing age and frailty. The harsh Yorkshire winters would be hard on her gran with her aching joints. How long did Lucas Rothwell expect her grandmother to wait on him hand and foot? Even though he spent less time at Rothwell Park than he had previously, it was ridiculous to expect a woman nudging eighty to remain in domestic service without help.

It was clear the castle was not being cleaned the way it used to be. Dust bunnies were in their dozens along the corridors, and cobwebs hung like lacework from the wall lights, as well as from the chandeliers. It gave the castle a ghostly atmosphere that was a little creepy to say the least. Surely Lucas could afford a team of people to run his damn castle. There were three gardeners, for God's sake. He had made a fortune as a landscape architect, working on massive projects all over Europe. Why not have three housekeepers?

There was a service lift to the upper storeys of the castle, but that was no help with the long corridors and galleries in each commodious wing. The library was in a wing all of its own, overlooking the rolling moors in the distance, divided here and there by dry stone walls and hedgerows. The door was closed, so Ruby placed the tray on a nearby hall table and then gave the door a light knock with her bent knuckles.

The *tap-tap-tap* sound echoed hauntingly along the wide corridor.

'Come in.'

The deep burr of Lucas Rothwell's voice sent a light shiver along the flesh of Ruby's arms and set those bats' wings in her belly flapping again. He could be intimidating at times, but she was no longer a timid child. She was a proud and successful business-woman, and she had an important busi-ness proposition to discuss. She would not be bashful around him now. She would be brusque and businesslike.

Game face on, Ruby turned the door han-dle and then picked up the tray and nudged the door further open in order to enter the library. But something stopped her going any further. The room—dark at the best of times, with all that ancient woodwork and the shelves stacked with valuable old books—was cast in long ghostly shadows.

Lucas was sitting with his back to her in one of the two wing chairs set in front of a quartet of tall narrow windows, situated be-tween sections of the floor-to-ceiling book-shelves. The sky outside had clouded over even more since her arrival—it was now a gunmetal-grey—and specks of rain hit the windows, pecking at the glass like tiny invisible beaks.

'Who is it?' Lucas's voice sharpened and he rose from the chair and turned to face where Ruby was standing in the doorway.

He was dressed in a black rollneck jumper and black trousers that made him seem even taller than his impressive six foot three. And he was wearing sunglasses, the aviator sort, which were as effective as a *Keep Out* sign. He cocked his head, his nostrils flaring slightly, like a wolf trying to pick up a new scent. *Her* scent.

The thought sent another shiver coursing over her flesh and a warm blush over her cheeks. If only she didn't blush so easily around him. What was it about Lucas Rothwell that made her feel like a gauche teenager instead of a fully grown adult?

The Embarrassing Incident—Ruby always capitalised it in her head—when she was sixteen was partly to blame. More than partly, if she was honest. Whenever she was in his presence—which was rare these days, thank God—she couldn't help but think of the clumsy, tipsy pass she'd made at him at one of the Rothwell parties she had sneaked into. And the stern dressing-down he'd given her that had rung in her ears for hours afterwards.

Eleven years had passed since that cringeworthy night, but it was as fresh in her mind as if it had happened yesterday. But she would *not* let it get in the way of achieving her goal. Harper and Aerin were relying on her to secure Rothwell Park as a wedding venue for Delphine Rainbird, a famous American actor, who was marrying her bodyguard, Miguel Morales. The exposure for their wedding business would be fantastic, let alone the amount of money Delphine was willing to pay to have her fairy tale wedding in a castle on the windswept moors of Yorkshire.

'If you'd turn a light on or take those sunglasses off, you'd see it's me.' Ruby carried the tray over to the table next to the wing chair he had just vacated. 'Why are you wearing them inside on a day like today? There's not exactly blinding sunshine coming through the windows.'

There was a beat or two of silence before he answered in a hollow tone. 'Headache.'

'Oh, sorry. I'll try not to rattle the cups too loudly.' She proceeded to pour the tea into the two cups, and the *glug-glug-*

glug sound in the silence was as loud as a waterfall.

'What are you doing?' His voice contained a note or two of irritation and his eyebrows were drawn together, his mouth pulled into a tight line. He remained standing in a stiff and guarded posture that was more than a little off-putting. But Ruby was not going to waste the opportunity to spend some time alone with him to present her proposal.

'I'm having afternoon tea with you. Anyway, you can't possibly eat all that parkin on your own.'

'Take it away. All of it. And close the door on your way out.' He turned his back on her and stood staring out of the rain-spattered windows, his hands thrust deep into the pockets of his trousers.

Ruby let out a long sigh. 'Look, I know headaches can make the most even-tempered person a little irritable, but I've come a long way and I'd like to talk to you about something. Something important.'

'Now's not a good time.'

'When would be a good time?'

There was another cavernous silence. The old bookshelves made a creaking sound, and the howling wind outside whipped up a few stray leaves on the ground and sent them past the windows in a whirligig.

Lucas finally released a long, ragged sigh and then lifted one of his hands out of his trouser pocket to rake it through his black hair, the tracks of his fingers leaving deep grooves in the thick strands.

'Is it about your grandmother?'

The quality of his tone had changed, the sharp edges softening slightly. He remained with his back to her, and the broadness of his shoulders and his strong spine tapering down to lean hips stirred a flicker of female awareness in her body. An awareness she didn't want to acknowledge, even to herself. Men like Lucas Rothwell were way out of her league. He only dated supermodels—not homely, girl-next-door-types with freckles and acne scars.

'Partly, yes.' Ruby figured discussing her gran would at least give her a good lead-in to her business proposal.

Lucas turned from the window and reached out with one of his hands for the back of the wing chair, lowering himself into it. He stretched his long legs out, crossing his feet at the ankles. His pose was casual, but she sensed a coiled tension in him. Was it because of his headache?

She couldn't remember him ever being ill. Was it a tension headache or a full-blown migraine? She had heard migraines made bright light unbearable to the sufferer and often caused vision disturbance. No wonder he was wearing sunglasses inside.

'You can pour.' He nodded in the direction of the tea tray.

If it hadn't been for his headache Ruby would have insisted he say please. While Lucas was taciturn and abrupt at the best of times, he was not normally flat-out rude. Well, not unless she was tipsy and begging him to kiss her. *Argh.* Why couldn't she blot out that wretched moment from her memory for good? On that occasion he had been brutally rude. And from that day her teenage crush had switched to a blistering loathing.

She'd avoided him for months after that, leaving a room as soon as she found him in it, or taking long, arduous detours across the moors if ever she saw him on one of her walks. By the time she was eighteen, she'd left to find work in London, only coming back to see her grandmother two or three times a year. Most of the time when she saw Lucas now he was in a gossip magazine, with yet another stunning woman draped over one of his arms. His success as an award-winning landscape architect saw him travelling the world for his high-end clients. He only visited Rothwell Park intermittently now, which meant she had to make the most of this time with him.

Ruby poured tea into the two cups. 'Do you still take it black, no sugar?'

'Yes.'

She handed him the cup, but his fingers fumbled against the saucer, which made some of the tea slosh over the side of the cup. He let out a curt swear-word, not quite under his breath, and quickly steadied the cup by holding his hand over the top.

'Sorry. Did it burn you?' he asked.

Ruby took her cup of tea and sat on the other wing chair. 'No, but speaking of burns… Have you seen the scald mark on my gran's wrist?'

Even though he was still wearing his aviator glasses she could see the lines of a frown form on his forehead. 'No. Is it bad?'

'I think she should see a doctor to have it properly assessed. I'm worried it might need a skin graft. But you know what she's like about seeking medical attention.'

'I do know,' Lucas said, his frown deepening into a two-pleat groove visible above the silver frames of his sunglasses.

'You can take a look at it and see for yourself. Maybe she'll listen to you rather than me.'

A flicker of tension flashed across his features. 'I have no experience with burns. But there's a first aid kit in the downstairs bathroom. A medical friend of mine put it together a while back. Feel free to help yourself.'

'Thank you. I'll see what I can do.' Ruby eyed the delicious parkin on the tray between them and her stomach gave an audible growl of hunger. 'Would you like some of Gran's parkin?'

'No, thank you. But you go ahead.'

Ruby took a slice of the rich black treacle, brown sugar and ginger treat and placed it on a plate. But then, suddenly self-conscious about eating in front of him, especially as he wasn't indulging, she put the plate to one side.

He frowned again. 'What's wrong?'

'I'll save it for later.'

He made a soft sound of impatience and placed his cup back on the table. 'Don't be ridiculous. Eat it. Isn't it your favourite?'

'Yes, and that's why I'd better not eat it. I won't be able to stop at one slice.'

One side of his mouth lifted in an indulgent-looking half-smile. It took years off his face and made him seem less brooding and intimidating. 'I thought you'd learned your lesson about overindulging?'

There was a mocking note in his tone that made her squirm in her chair. Ruby could feel a hot blush crawling over her cheeks and buried her face in her teacup, taking a sip or two before changing the subject.

'I have a favour to ask.'

She put the cup and saucer down, and was annoyed she couldn't control the tiny rattle of crockery. It betrayed her nerves, as if she was still that gauche, hero-worshipping, knobbly-kneed schoolgirl.

'I have a celebrity client who wants to get married in Yorkshire and—'

'No.' The flatly delivered negative cut through the air like a gunshot and his expression closed like a shutter slamming.

'But you haven't let me finish—'

Lucas put his cup on the table, rose from his chair and moved back to stand in front of the windows, his back turned towards her again. 'It's out of the question.'

The intractable edge to his tone sent a

ripple of anger through her. She *had* to sell the proposal to him. So much depended on her securing Rothwell Park as a wedding venue. Her business partners were depending on her to nail this location for their client. She couldn't let them down. Harper and Aerin were her family now. Failure wasn't an option. Failing was what her mother did, not her. Ruby set goals and achieved them. She made plans and carried them out. She made promises she delivered on without fail.

'But why?'

Lucas gave a grunt of humourless laughter. 'You mean apart from me loathing weddings?'

Ruby let out a gusty sigh. 'Not all weddings are like your parents' ones. I mean, not many couples get married to and divorced from each other three times.'

He turned around to face her, his expression etched in intractable lines. 'You're wasting your time, Ruby. I won't budge on this.'

And there she was thinking her grandmother was stubborn. Lucas took obstinacy to a whole new level. Seriously, he made the most obstinate mule look like a pushover.

'But Rothwell Park is the perfect setting

for a wedding. There's so much space and the huge kitchen is a dream to work in. My friend Harper is desperate to photograph the wedding here. The gothic setting really appeals to her. Remember you met her once when she came to visit me here? We met in care. And the wedding planner, Aerin, will organise everything, so there's nothing you'll have to do. She's such a perfectionist—nothing will be left to chance. You wouldn't even have to be here. I'll bring my catering team in a few days early to set up. Please, Lucas, at least think about it before you say—'

'No.'

Ruby sprang from her chair, almost knocking the tea tray off the table. She stood in front of him with her hands balled into tight fists, anger stiffening her spine and frustration heating her cheeks. She couldn't let him stand in the way of her goal. She couldn't let him thwart her carefully, meticulously laid-out plans. She couldn't allow him to make her break her promise to her friends and their celebrity client. The wedding *had* to go ahead. She would find a way to convince him, even if it took longer than the weekend.

She. Could. Not. Fail.

'I can't believe you're being so unfair. This wedding is the biggest we've ever done and it will boost our profile so much. All those rooms are lying vacant upstairs. We could house all the guests—some of them very important people. Do you realise the revenue we could raise from this? It's a dream come true for—'

Lucas turned back to the bleak view of the brooding sky. 'Please leave.'

'No. I will *not* damn well leave.'

Before she could stop herself, Ruby placed one of her hands on his arm to force him to face her. He jolted as if she had touched him with a live wire. A tingling sensation travelled along the length of her own arm and she was acutely conscious of the firm male muscles tensing under her hold.

She couldn't recall touching him since that awful night when she was sixteen. But the electric sensation was exactly the same. A strange fizzing energy that sent tiny buzzing pulses along the network of her nerves. She was standing so close to his imposing height it sent her heart into a crazy hit-and-miss rhythm. The citrus and woodsy notes of his aftershave teased her senses into a stupor. Although he clearly hadn't shaved for a week, possibly more, and the rich dark stubble peppering his strong jaw and growing around his sculpted mouth gave him a rakish look.

Eek! Why had she looked at his mouth?

The top lip was slightly thinner than the bottom, their vermilion borders and the philtrum ridge between his nose and top lip so well defined they could have been carved by Michelangelo. It was a mouth that had inspired many a teenage fantasy. And all these years later Ruby still wondered what those firm lips would feel like against her own. Hard and insistent? Soft and sensually persuasive? Or something irresistibly in between?

Lucas placed his broad-spanned hand over hers and lifted it off his arm as if it was speck of lint. 'Do you really think that tactic is going to work?'

His tone was liberally laced with scorn and another wave of heat flowed to her cheeks.

Ruby glowered up at him, but all she could see was her own furious reflection in his aviator glasses. 'Firstly, I'm not leaving until you agree to hear me out. And secondly, I can't leave my gran struggling all by herself with a burned wrist. Why haven't you engaged another housekeeper? This place is clearly too much for her now.'

'She insists she doesn't want to retire.'

'But can't you see how neglected this place is at the moment? There are cobwebs everywhere.'

His mouth went into a thin tight line. 'No, I *can't* see.'

Something about his bleak-sounding tone made Ruby frown. 'But there's heaps of them. Look at that one at the top of the window, and on the light there. You'd have to blind not to see them.'

The line of his mouth became embittered. 'But that's exactly my point—I am blind.'

CHAPTER TWO

LUCAS HEARD RUBY'S sucked-in breath and the sound of her gripping the back of one of the wing chairs as if his news had shocked her to the core. But then, when he'd been hit with his diagnosis just over a month ago he'd been knocked sideways too.

Even if he did fully regain his sight, post-surgery, how was he supposed to juggle his work commitments in the meantime? How was he going to manage day-to-day life? He was not the type of man to depend on others for anything. He was fiercely, ruth-lessly independent and could not imagine any other way of living.

'Blind?' Ruby gasped. 'But how? I mean, what happened?'

'I had a pituitary tumour removed last month.'

'A tumour? Was it...*malignant*?' She

whispered the word, as if it terrified her to say it out loud.

'Thankfully, no. But the surgery resulted in considerable swelling against the optic nerve.'

He heard the sound of Ruby swallowing and the creak of a floorboard, as if she was shifting her weight from foot to foot. He could imagine her small white teeth pulling at her plump lower lip and his blood thickened and drummed softly, deep and low in his body. It was a faint pulse that strengthened into a pounding beat as his mind kept running with memories of her understated beauty.

Touching her had been a mistake. An error of judgement that had caught him off guard. *She'd* caught him off guard. The smell of her—the intoxicating peony and tuberose and summer scent he always associated with her—made him want to get closer to her, to breathe her.

Why was he so aware of her all of a sudden? It made no sense. He had done his best to ignore her since she was a kid—especially since that night of the party. Her sixteen-year-old schoolgirl crush might have been flattering to some, but to him it had reinforced his conviction that infatuation masquerading as love was a disaster waiting to happen. His parents had demonstrated that three times with their rollercoaster relationship that consisted of passionately falling in and out of love.

That day he had made it clear to Ruby where the boundaries lay. Those boundaries had been in place for eleven years and he was determined they would stay that way.

'Is it…permanent? I mean, your loss of sight?'

'My specialist is cautiously optimistic. Usually sight does return, but in rare instances it doesn't.' Lucas released a breath he hadn't been aware of holding and added, 'I can see shapes, but there's no definition. And light and dark. But that's about all.'

'I'm so sorry… And here I was, gabbling on about blinding sunshine and why can't you see the cobwebs. Oh, God, I'm *so* sorry.' The anguish in her voice was palpable.

He pictured her cherry-red cheeks and in spite of everything smiled to himself. He had never met a young woman who blushed so much. Those fiery blushes made her freckles stand out like nutmeg sprinkled on a dessert. 'Please. Stop apologising.'

There was a loaded silence.

Lucas was aware of every breath she took, every movement she made. The rustle of her clothes, the squeak of her shoes, the swish of her fragrant hair. Aware of her in a way he had never been before. Or maybe that was because he'd been alone for weeks without a visitor, apart from the occupational therapist who had taught him how to navigate his surroundings and manage basic tasks such as dressing and eating and drinking.

While the OT had been excellent at her job, he still occasionally bumped into furniture, and the last thing he wanted was anyone witnessing it. He'd given his housekeeper, Beatrice Pennington, strict instructions to keep all visitors away. But he hadn't realised Beatrice had injured herself. But then how could he have? He couldn't see a damn thing, and she was loyal to a fault—the type who wouldn't dream of letting him down at his lowest point.

'Lucas... I meant what I said about Gran. I'll have to stay a few days to help her. And if I can talk her into retiring, then I can help you interview new applicants and—'

'I don't want anyone else here while I'm recuperating,' Lucas said, barely able to keep his tone civil.

The thought of his trustworthy house-keeper retiring was out of the question for now. How could he protect his privacy with strangers traipsing about the castle? He only needed another month or two to see how his sight was progressing.

'The whole point of me being here is to keep my condition out of the press. As far as I'm concerned, the press have had their fair share of Rockwell scandals to report. I will not allow myself to become yet an-other one of them.'

'But Gran needs—'

'I understand you're worried about your grandmother. Take her to a doctor for treat-ment, but you'll have to leave after that. I'm not interested in replacing her until my sight returns.'

If my sight returns.

He didn't say the words, but they hov-ered in the air like some of those cobwebs she'd mentioned.

Ruby gave a heavy sigh and he heard her clothes rustle again, as if her shoulders had slumped. 'You can't stay holed up here for ever. You have a business to run and so do I—which brings me back to Delphine Rain-bird's wedding.'

Lucas ground his teeth. 'How I run my

business is no concern of yours. And I've already given you my answer about the wedding.'

'But you don't understand how important this is to me.'

The pleading note in her voice was almost his undoing. Almost. But the last thing he wanted was a media circus at his private residence. Paparazzi and drones and helicopters trying to get the money shot. He was a private man at the best of times. What the press would make of his loss of sight was anyone's guess, but he was not going to do anything to risk exposure.

His childhood had been full of media intrusions as journalists had tried to get the latest on his parents—either their recoupling or their uncoupling. Some of the press had even taken to tailing him, asking for a comment on his parents' current relationship status. Not only had it embarrassed him, it had made him determined never to allow his emotions to become so out of control that the press would find any relationship he conducted newsworthy.

As if that had worked. He loathed the way the press was always tagging him, speculating on his love-life, documenting his every move.

'I'm sorry to disappoint you but it's not going to happen. You'll have to find somewhere else.'

'But there's nowhere quite like Rothwell Park. It's got such a wonderfully gothic atmosphere, and I know it'll make Delphine's wedding all the more spectacular—especially with Harper's photography. Delphine came here as a child with her parents, to one of your parents' parties. It left a big impression on her and she's dreamed of being married here ever since. Some of the world's biggest celebrities will be coming—possibly even royalty. It might bring Harper and Aerin and I more high-end clients. In fact, we're counting on it. This is what we need to lift our business to the next level.'

Lucas tried not to imagine Ruby's imploring expression, but it filled his imagination regardless. A beseeching spaniel had nothing on her. He could picture her toffee-brown eyes, fringed with thick long lashes and framed by dark eyebrows. Her full-lipped mouth—no doubt downturned at the corners right now—her ski slope nose, her high cheekbones...

She wasn't classically beautiful, more understated girl-next-door than over-the-top glamourous. She lightened her mid-brown hair to blonde, but her roots nearly always grew through an inch or two before she got around to touching them up. He often wondered if she coloured her hair so she didn't resemble her mother, who had chosen a life of crime over her. Ruby wore the bare minimum of make-up and mostly casual clothes. She was proud and feisty and she had a streak of obstinacy—no doubt inherited from her grandmother.

But Lucas could be stubborn too. And on this issue, he was not going to budge. 'I hate to disappoint you, but there's not going to be another wedding at Rothwell Park while I'm the owner. Do I make myself crystal-clear?'

'I can understand why you want your privacy. I'd be the same. But I need this wedding so badly.'

He heard her proceeding to load their cups and saucers back on the tray, her movements ordered and methodical, but he sensed her frustration all the same.

'What am I supposed to tell my friends?' Her lowered tone made it sound as if the question was addressed to herself rather than him. 'I can't let them down... I promised.'

The teaspoons clinked against the saucers and he heard her let out a long-winded sigh. Lucas knew all about broken promises. His parents had made numerous promises to each other, and to him, and they had all been broken. Some faster than others, but still ultimately broken.

'I'm sorry, Ruby, but you shouldn't have made a promise before you were absolutely certain you could honour it.'

'But all you have to say is yes and I *will* be able to honour it. You're standing in the way of my success. And I know you're only doing it because of—'

He heard her suck in her breath, as if she had decided not to continue with her rant.

'Because of…?'

The things on the tray rattled as she picked it up from the table. 'Because of what happened all those years ago.'

'Nothing happened.'

Lucas had made absolutely sure of that. Yes, he had been a little brutal in telling her how inappropriately she had behaved, but back then the seven years difference in their ages back had been a chasm that couldn't and shouldn't have been bridged.

'I suppose I should thank you for not taking advantage of me.'

'Perhaps I should apologise for being a little curt with you.'

There was a pulsing silence.

Ruby drew in a breath and released it on a stuttering sigh. 'I'm not going to give up, you know.'

The steely thread of determination was back in her voice.

'Neither am I.'

He could sense her eyes on him. He could see the vague outline of her standing stiffly in front of him, with the tray in her hands. He wished he could see her face, see those flashing toffee-brown eyes and the shape of her lips. But wishing was not going to bring his eyesight back. Only time could do that.

Ruby left the library and took the tray back to the kitchen. Thankfully, her gran wasn't there, so she'd have some time to process her thoughts over Lucas's revelation.

It was such a shock to think of him without his sight. To think of a man who had built a global career on constructing beautiful gardens for his clients no longer being able to see anything but vague shapeless outlines.

He was a proud man who had locked

himself away from the public eye while he waited to see if his eyesight would return.

What if it didn't?

Her heart squeezed at the thought of him robbed of such a vital sense. How would he run his business? How would he be able to design gardens if he could only see shapes but no definition? He was a man who attended to detail. He was meticulous and thorough in all he did. Now it all hung in the balance while he waited to find out if his sight would return.

She mentally retraced every word of her interaction with him and a wave of shame coursed through her. If she hadn't been so focussed on delivering her proposal she might have picked up on the clues a little earlier. He was wearing sunglasses. He was sitting in the darkened library with no book in his hands or on the table beside his chair. There was not a mobile phone or laptop in sight—things that rarely left his side when he was working on multiple projects.

He had touched her hand whilst reaching for the teacup.

He'd touched her...

Ruby looked down at her hand and flexed her fingers where his hand had so briefly lain. A shiver shimmied down her spine and she closed her hand into a fist, trying to stop the fizzing sensation that lingered in her flesh from the heat of his touch.

She gave herself a stern mental shake and left the kitchen to fetch the first aid kit from the downstairs bathroom. She opened the bathroom door, but then caught a glimpse of herself in the gilt-edged mirror over the basin and suppressed a groan at the sight of her pink cheeks.

She wasn't the blushing sort when it came to interacting with men.

But with Lucas…

Ruby released a shuddering sigh and pulled open the cupboard below the basin to find the kit. She had to get a grip on herself. Because she was not leaving Rothwell Park until she had his agreement on the wedding, and nor was she leaving her gran on her own. Leaving without his agreement would be failing—and she could not fail.

This wedding was her chance—to help expand Happy Ever After Weddings This was her chance to build the sort of financial security that would allow her to put her poverty-stricken past well and truly behind her. The potential was at her fingertips, and she couldn't allow Lucas to snatch it away from her.

Besides, Lucas clearly needed more support than he was currently receiving. She could offer it at the same time as helping her gran…

Ruby found her gran in the sitting room in the servants' quarters. It was only used by Beatrice these days, and was comfortable in a spartan way, which was how her gran preferred it.

'You could've given me the heads-up about Lucas's condition,' Ruby said, and set the first aid kit on the lamp table next to her gran's armchair.

'It's not my place to be revealing the master's private information.'

'I would never tell anyone.'

Her gran narrowed her eyes. 'What about those friends of yours? And all those social media things you're on? One slip of the tongue and the world's press would be on the doorstep.'

'They won't hear it from me.'

Ruby opened the first aid kit and took out antiseptic wash and some cotton wool pads.

If by some miracle Delphine's wedding went ahead, the world's press would indeed be on the doorstep. But there was no point discussing that with her gran—not until she was sure Lucas could be won over.

Her gran winced as Ruby wrapped a crepe bandage around her wrist. 'Not too tight,' she said through pinched lips.

Ruby unwound the bandage a little, a frown tugging at her brow. 'I'm going to take you to the doctor right now. The sooner you have this seen to, the sooner it will get better. You can't risk losing your arm.'

'Don't be daft. I won't be losing my arm…' But her gran's tone had a tremulous note of worry in it that hadn't been there before.

Ruby secured the bandage and met her gran's troubled gaze. 'This has to be seen to today. I've done first aid, Gran, so I know a bad burn when I see it.'

Within a short time Ruby had made an appointment with the local doctor, who advised her to pack a bag for her gran in case she needed to be admitted to hospital. Another hour or so later, once Beatrice had been assessed by a no-nonsense doctor who had advised intravenous antibiotics and a hospital stay of at least a week, Ruby drove back to Rothwell Park, comforted that her gran was finally receiving the medical attention she needed.

Before informing Lucas of her gran's hospital stay, Ruby took her phone upstairs to her room, so she could have a three-way call with her business partners.

'I'm going to have to stay a little longer than I thought. My gran has been admitted to hospital for treatment for a burn.'

Although she wanted to tell the girls about Lucas's situation, and implicitly trusted their discretion, she could not bear to betray his trust.

'Oh, your poor gran. Is she going to be okay?' Aerin asked.

'She'll be fine if she does what she's told. The doctor wants to keep her in for a few days for the antibiotics to do their job. Gran wasn't happy about it, but I managed to talk her round.'

'Did you ask Lucas about Delphine's wedding?' Harper asked, and the eagerness in her voice made Ruby feel awful for not being transparent about the situation.

'Yes, but I'm still negotiating with him.'

'I'm not sure I like the sound of that,' Harper said. 'We need to lock in the date as soon as possible. Delphine has her heart set on Rothwell Park. It's perfect in every way. She wants the guests to stay on site, and the castle is big enough to accommodate everyone—including her security team. Besides, I want the photos I can take there for the website.'

'I can't plan anything until we know for sure,' Aerin said with a hint of panic in her tone. 'We're on a tight timeline in any case. And it's a remote location, so things will take more time than—'

'I know, but leave it with me. I think I can convince him.'

Ruby wasn't feeling as confident as she sounded to her friends, but her determination more than made up for that. She had to find a way to convince Lucas that holding the wedding at Rothwell Park would be a win-win situation. It was going to be a hard sell to someone who was almost phobic about weddings, but still, it was worth a try.

Lucas was making his way upstairs to his suite of rooms when he heard the sound of the stairs above him creaking. The sound of Ruby's light footsteps as she approached him sent a frisson of awareness through his body. The fragrance of her wafted in front of his nostrils, making him want to press his face to the side of her slim neck and breathe her in.

Rein it in, buddy. He gave himself a stern talking-to. *She's off limits. She's always been off limits.*

'How's your grandmother? Did you take her to see the doctor? I heard your car leave a while back.'

'The doctor had admitted her to hospital to administer IV antibiotics.'

Lucas frowned. 'For how long?'

'A week.'

He drew in a breath and released it in a slow stream. 'I'm sorry I didn't realise her burn was as serious as that.'

He'd always prided himself on taking care of his staff, from the most senior to the most junior. It frustrated him that Beatrice, his most loyal staff member of all, had hurt herself and he had known nothing.

'Of course this changes everything.'

Ruby's voice contained an element of *I-told-you-so* that jangled at his already over-stretched nerves.

'Everything…?'

'I'll have to stay longer than the weekend. You'll need help while Gran's away, and—'

'I will not need help.'

The last thing he wanted was Ruby waiting on him hand and foot. It was bad enough having her here for the weekend. Seven days of trying to avoid her would be unbearable.

'Don't be silly, Lucas, of course you'll need help. I can work remotely for the next week. I can get the castle in some sort of order while Gran has a much-needed rest.'

Lucas saw the sense in her argument, but he also saw the pitfalls if he were to agree—which he was strangely tempted to do. Ruby was not the sort of person he could easily ignore. But wouldn't a week with her be preferable to a stranger filling in for his housekeeper?

'Fine. Stay, then. But I don't want to be disturbed unnecessarily. And once the week is up you'll have to leave.'

'Thanks for being so terribly gracious about it.'

Lucas could hear the sarcasm in her tone and imagined the pert tilt of her chin and the flash of her toffee-brown eyes. 'You're welcome.'

He moved up another step, and he sensed her on the one above him. He could smell not just her perfume but the fragrance of her hair—an apple and vanilla scent that teased his senses all over again. He could hear the soft sound of her indrawn breath and pictured her blinking at him with those wide puppy dog eyes. The desire to touch her shocked him to the core of his being. He had to tighten his hold on the balustrade and keep his other hand pressed against his right side.

'Excuse me. I want to go upstairs to bed.' He spoke through tight lips.

'Lucas?'

Her hand came down on his arm and a wave of heat travelled through his body in a blood-tingling current.

She took her hand away, as if she too felt that electric charge.

'It's way too early to go to bed. You need to have proper nutrition and exercise. And regular exposure to daylight so your circadian rhythms don't go out of whack. I can help you with that.'

'If you think your playing nursemaid is going to change my mind about the wedding, think again.'

He brushed past her but he heard her following him, her footsteps light but determined.

'Forget about the wedding for now. I'm doing this for Gran. I had no idea she wasn't keeping up with things the way she used to. I should've come back before this to check on her. I shouldn't have relied on phone calls. I should have come in person.'

Self-recrimination laced her voice, and it triggered his own gut-clawing guilt.

Lucas stopped walking up the stairs and turned in Ruby's direction. 'It's not your fault. If it's anyone's, it's mine. But with my operation and all, I just—'

'You mustn't blame yourself. Gran is a stubborn old goat who wouldn't listen until I told her the arm was likely to be amputated if the infection got any worse.'

'It won't come to that, surely?'

'Let's hope not.'

'It seems your visit was timely.'

'Yes...'

Lucas knew how much Beatrice missed Ruby, although she never let on. It wasn't the housekeeper's way to wear her heart on her sleeve. But he was feeling a little uncomfortable that she hadn't told him about her injury. Her loyalty was admirable, and her stoicism something he had always admired, but he was her employer and ultimately responsible for her welfare.

He hated it that he was unable to conduct his life the way he wanted. This loss of control was anathema to him. It reminded him of the chaotic rollercoaster of living with his parents as they fell in and out of love with each other repeatedly. One minute they would be passionately in love and all would be well, and then the fights would start. Horrible fights, with cruel insults hurled and doors slammed and voices raised. Then, after his father had moved out—or his mother, depending on who had had the latest affair in order to wound the other—the cycle would begin again.

Sometimes the peace had lasted for so long he'd lower his guard. He'd be lulled into thinking that this time they were going to make it and all would be well. But of course he was always disappointed.

Lucas had learned the hard way not to trust their passion or their promises. A cynical crust had formed around his heart and he longer believed in lasting love. He went into his short flings with his eyes wide open and his guard up.

And that wasn't going to change any time soon.

CHAPTER THREE

Ruby watched as Lucas climbed the stairs to his suite of rooms, torn between wanting to follow him and needing to keep her distance. At least he'd agreed to let her stay the week, but his stubbornness over her helping him in any way was beyond frustrating. It was also imperative she got him to agree to host Delphine's wedding, but how could she change his mind?

She might not like him much, but she'd have to have a heart as hard and cold as marble not to feel empathy for his situation. He had always struck her as a bit of a loner. He was not like his extroverted parents in any way other than having the same good looks as his father. She didn't even know if he saw his father these days. His mother had died of a brain tumour a few years ago, and his father had remarried within a couple of months and promptly created a new family with a much younger wife in Brazil.

Ruby sighed and went back down to the kitchen to see about dinner. Cooking for her was not just work or even a hobby—it was her happy place. Preparing ingredients, using her creativity to develop new tastes and flavours, brought her immense satisfaction. Her busy life running the wedding business with her friends left little time for a social life, but she didn't let it worry her. She liked the security it gave her to know she was earning her own money and not being dependent on others as her mother had been.

Which was why securing Rothwell Park for Delphine's wedding was of paramount importance to her right now. Convincing Lucas to allow it to go ahead was going to be a big challenge, but never let it be said that she had ever backed down from a challenge.

The bigger the better.

A couple of hours later, Ruby set up the smaller of the two dining rooms for Lucas's meal. She went up the stairs to the master bedroom and rapped her knuckles on the door.

'Lucas? Dinner is ready downstairs.'

She heard him let out a curse word and then the sound of his firm tread as he came to the door. He opened it and stood there glaring down at her—without his sunglasses this time. The outer rims of his irises were a dark smoky grey, the centre an ice-floe-blue with ink-black pupils. His lashes were long and thick, his eyebrows prominent. His hair was tousled, as if he had been raking his hands through it, but if anything it made him look even more attractive. He had taken off his shoes, but he still towered over her.

'I thought I told you I wasn't hungry?'

'And I told you how important it is to eat well. A good diet will help your recovery.'

He gave a rough-edged sigh and his hand fell away from where it was gripping the door. 'I never knew you could be so persistent. I'll be down in a minute. I need to put on my shoes.'

Ruby could have gone ahead and got ready to serve dinner, but she stayed in the open doorway, watching as he tried to locate his shoes. He bumped his foot against the bedside table and let out another colourful curse.

'Damn it to hell.'

'They're over here.'

Ruby went to where the shoes were half pushed under the bed. It wasn't the first time she had entered his room—during her girlhood crush she had slipped in unnoticed several times. Her cheeks warmed as those memories resurfaced. She had been so infatuated with Lucas, so desperately in love with him—or at least with the version of him her teenage mind had conjured. She bent down to pull his shoes out from under the bed, and then straightened and brought them to him. She crouched in in front of him and set them next to the socked toes of his left foot.

You are not going to think about the fact you are on your knees in front of Lucas Rothwell. Gulp. In his bedroom.

Ruby wouldn't have wished blindness on anyone, but right then, with her cheeks hot enough to solve an energy crisis, she was glad he couldn't see her blush.

'Here you go.'

Lucas slipped his feet into the shoes and gave a grimace. 'Thanks...'

Ruby straightened in front of him, conscious of how close they were standing to each other. Never had she been so aware of a man. Of his power and potency. Of his commanding presence and how it affected her. Her body tingled from head to foot. Even the roots of her hair lifted away from the skin of her scalp. Her heart began to beat a little faster—a staccato rhythm that banged against her breastbone and made it hard for her to draw another breath. She knew she should step back, put some distance between them before she was tempted to touch him.

Don't even think about touching him.

But for some strange reason she was unable to step back. Her feet were nailed to the floor by an invisible force she had no way of counteracting.

Time seemed to stand still. The silence stretched. Her heart hammered like the piston in a faulty engine.

Lucas lifted his hand to her face, touching her cheek with the lightest touch, his fingers ever so slowly trailing down to the base of her chin. So close...so *achingly* close to her lower lip that her mouth buzzed and fizzed and tingled in anticipation. She drew in a soft breath and his hand fell away as if her skin had burned him.

'Forgive me.' His tone was so rough he could have been gargling with gravel.

'It's okay...'

Ruby couldn't seem to get her voice above a whisper, or get her heartrate to slow down to anywhere near normal. Her heart was bouncing up and down in her chest cavity as if it was on a pogo stick. His touch had been so light, but it had created a firestorm in her flesh. Stirrings and yearnings and urgings were erupting in places she didn't want to think about. Places she *forbade* herself to think about. The one time she had touched him in the past it had turned into the most humiliating experience of her life.

Lucas stepped away, his forehead cast in a severe frown. 'It's not okay. You have my word it won't happen again.'

I want it to happen again.

Ruby was shocked at where her mind was leading her. Shocked and ashamed and furious with herself. For years she had done everything in her power to avoid touching him. But now the desire—the fervent, aching desire—to touch him beat in her fingertips like a primitive drum. It was an ache in her flesh, an urgent ache to feel his hand gliding down her face. And not just her face but other places on her body. Touching her, exploring her, pleasuring her...

She suppressed a tiny shudder. 'I guess

you have to use your other senses to make up for your loss of sight. Touch is one way of knowing how someone looks or what expression they have on their face.'

'I don't have to touch your face to read the pity that's likely there.' His tone was embittered and his expression dark and brooding.

'You think I pity you? If I do, it's not because of your lack of sight. It's because you're refusing to make what you can of your life at present. Thousands—no, millions of people are blind and live happy, fulfilled lives.'

'Please spare me the lecture on how I should live my life.' He spoke the words through white tight lips.

Ruby let out a long sigh. 'I know this must be an awful time for you. Everything has happened so suddenly and, just like after any surgery, it'll take some time to get used to your new circumstances. Everything must seem out of whack for you right now. And I want to help you get through it. But I can't do that if you aren't prepared to meet me halfway.'

'I don't need your help.'

'When was the last time you shaved?'

A savage frown carved deep on his forehead. 'What?'

Ruby stepped up close to him again and lifted her hand to his stubbly jaw. He flinched as if her touch burned him, but he didn't step away. She placed her hand back on his face, gliding it over the rough regrowth. The raspy sound was loud in the silence. She lowered her hand from his face and tried to ignore the fluttery sensation in her belly. Tried to ignore the tingling in her fingers and the pulse of something dark and silky and secretive between her thighs.

'Unless you intend to grow a beard, you really could do with a shave. I could drive you to a barber, if you like.'

'I'm not going anywhere.'

'I could maybe get one to do a house call.'

'No.' He moved away to search for his sunglasses on the bedside table. He slipped them on and turned to face her with an unreadable expression. 'What? Not going to offer to shave me yourself?'

Ruby could feel another blush crawling over her cheeks. 'I can't imagine you allowing me to come at you with a razor in my hand. Who knows what might happen?'

One side of his mouth lifted at the corner. 'Who, indeed.'

Something about his sardonic tone sent a shiver rolling down her spine and Ruby turned for the door before she was tempted to touch him again. What was wrong with her? Did she have no shame—especially after the blistering set-down he'd given her all those years ago? She had to get a hold of herself. The last thing she needed right now was the complication of developing an attraction to the one man who would never be interested in someone like her.

A few minutes later they were seated in the dining room. Ruby dished up a portion of the casserole she had made onto his plate and filled his glass with wine.

'Bon appetit.'

Lucas leaned down to sniff the steam rising off his plate. 'Mmm, smells good.' His fingers briefly searched for cutlery. He cocked his head, as if sensing she was watching him. 'Is something wrong?'

She flicked her napkin across her lap and picked up her own cutlery. 'It must have been hard to learn how to eat without vision'

'I'm getting used to it.' A frown flitted

across his brow and he added, 'I had the help of a very efficient occupational therapist for a couple of weeks.'

'That must have been a great help.'

'She's the mother of three adult children and has zero tolerance for self-pity.' One side of his mouth tilted in an almost-smile, which was a little rueful around the edges. 'I told her she'd missed a great career in the army as a drill sergeant.'

'You won't have been an easy client.'

His smile dropped away and he moved the food around his plate, a brooding frown pulling on his brow. 'No, I wasn't.'

'Why did you come back here to recuperate?' Ruby asked. 'I mean, you hardly spend any time here these days. I got the impression you didn't enjoy being here.'

He put down his fork and picked up his wine glass. 'I chose it because of the isolation. The press would have a field-day if they found out about my condition. Plus, I know my way around here. I spent my childhood seeking out various hiding places to avoid the battles between my parents.' He took a sip of his wine and put the glass back down, the line of his mouth bitter. 'I don't remember this place as a home. It was more of a war zone.'

'But your parents weren't always unhappy. I remember them being so in love and—'

'I hardly think that was *love*.' Cynicism was ripe in his tone. 'They lived off each other's drama. They got high on it. They weren't happy unless they were making each other unhappy.' He shook his head, as if he still couldn't make sense of his parents' relationship. 'If that's what love is, I want no part of it.'

'Have you ever been in love?'

'No.'

'But you've dated so many women. Hasn't one of them made you feel something?'

'Sure—but lust isn't love.' He picked up his wine glass again. 'I don't stay with anyone long enough to develop feelings for them.'

'But what if they develop feelings for you?'

'I don't intentionally set out to break anyone's heart. I state my terms and those who can handle them accept them.'

'It sounds like plenty of women do accept them.'

Ruby tried but failed to keep the note of disapproval out of her voice. If what was reported in the press was true, Lucas changed partners faster than a racing driver changed gears.

Lucas took another sip of his wine before answering. 'So, you're not a fan of casual hook-ups?' he asked.

Her cheeks grew warm. 'I have the occasional fling.'

'But you've never fallen in love.'

'Not yet.'

'But you'd like to.'

'Of course,' Ruby said. 'I work in the wedding industry. I would be a hypocrite if I didn't believe in love and want it for myself. I just haven't been lucky enough to find it yet. Nor have either of my business partners, Aerin and Harper—which is kind of ironic, really.'

Lucas made a sound that sounded like a *more-fool-you* snort. He picked up his cutlery again and ate a couple of mouthfuls. But then he paused with his fork halfway to his mouth, as if sensing her watching him. 'Look—I'm sorry about your grandmother. I hope she's going to be okay. If there's anything she needs, or if I can help in any way—'

Ruby reached for her glass of wine. 'Thank you, but I'm sure she'll be fine. Although I still think she needs to be encouraged to retire. She can't work for ever.'

There was a small silence.

Ruby studied his expression, wondering what was going on behind his shuttered features. He was hard to read at the best of times, but now he seemed even more closed off. He wouldn't be human if he wasn't worried about regaining his sight, but she sensed it was more than that. He had a big international business to run, staff to look after, multiple projects running at the same time. Yet he was unable to travel now—or at least chose not to until he was confident of a full recovery. No wonder there were lines of worry about his mouth and eyes that had not been there before.

'That's a conversation I intend to have with her sooner rather than later,' Lucas said. 'And it's another reason you can't host your client's wedding here.'

He paused as if expecting her to join the dots.

A stone landed in Ruby's stomach as she finally did. She put her wine glass down and stared at him. 'You're not thinking of... *selling* Rockwell Park?'

Even saying the word out loud seemed like sacrilege—like shouting a curse in the middle of a church service. This had been her only stable home, and she hated the thought of not being able to return to it. It was her base, the anchor that had kept her safe after bobbing up and down in the turbulent waters of her early childhood.

If Lucas sold it, she would never walk through the castle and its grounds again, never wander through the gardens and the moors beyond. A deep sense of loss assailed her—a sense that nothing would ever be the same again. She would not only be losing her sanctuary but a part of herself as well.

'It's too big for one person,' Lucas said, shrugging one shoulder in a dispassionate way. 'I spend most of my time abroad these days, so it makes sense to offload it to someone who'll make better use of it.'

Ruby opened and closed her mouth like a stranded fish gasping for air. 'But it's your home. The home of your ancestors. And, wait—what does your father think of you selling?'

'He signed over the deeds to me upon my mother's death. He has no wish ever to return to England, let alone live here, and nor does his young wife. She finds it too cold.'

Ruby bit her lip, still struggling to get her head around the fact Rothwell Park would not be a part of her life any more. She might not visit more than two or three times a year, but just knowing it was there, that her gran was there, gave her a sense of security.

She hadn't realised how much she'd clung to it until now. Having her beloved sanctuary taken away would be like revisiting the worst of her childhood—the constant moves from bedsit to bedsit as her mother tried to escape yet another unsavoury boyfriend or a drug debt that had got out of hand.

'But what's going to happen to my grandmother? She's lived her for so long.'

'You're the one who's insisting she needs to retire. I'll give her a generous pay-out, of course. And provide her with accommodation for the rest of her life.'

It was a more than generous offer, but Ruby still didn't understand why he was so intent on offloading Rothwell Park. How soon did he plan to sell it? Was selling it just something he was mulling over in his mind while he recuperated, or did he have a timeline in place?

'When do you intend to tell her?'

'Once the sale is finalised.'

Ruby's heart clanged against her breastbone. 'You mean you already have a buyer?'

Lucas's expression flickered with a hint of irritation. 'Why all the drama? It's an offer I'd be a fool to knock back.'

'So, it's all about the money.' It was a statement, not a question—a statement that burned in her throat like a searing hot coal. 'I thought you were nothing like your father, and yet here you are selling your birthright to the highest bidder.'

Lucas leaned back in his chair and curled his top lip in a cynical manner. 'You're welcome to make a counter-offer. The final contract is yet to be signed.'

She glared at him, even though she knew he couldn't see the blistering fire in her eyes. 'You know I haven't got that sort of money.'

And nor would she ever have that sort of money if she couldn't build the business to the heights she and her friends had planned. She swallowed the choking lump in her throat, determined to show no emotion in front of him.

'Ruby.'

His stern schoolmaster tone ignited her anger all over again.

'You're a successful businesswoman. You should know the importance of keeping emotion out of business deals.'

'But don't you feel *anything* for Rothwell Park? Anything at all?'

His features were as hard and cold as one of the marble busts of his ancestors in the gallery. 'As far as I'm concerned, this place is cursed.'

She frowned so hard it hurt her forehead. 'Cursed?'

The cynical twist to his mouth reappeared and he put his fork down with a hard little thud. 'You witnessed it yourself. My parents falling in and out of love. Breaking up and breaking each other. This place reminds me of nothing but angst and ill-feeling. I want nothing more to do with it.'

Ruby gaped at him. 'And you think that's Rothwell Park's fault? It was your parents and their hang-ups that cursed their relationship. It had nothing to do with this lovely old castle and its grounds. It's the people who make a place a home—not the bricks and mortar. Besides, when they were happy, they were truly happy. I have never seen two people more passionately in love with each other.'

Lucas gave a harsh laugh that was nowhere in the vicinity of humour. 'In love? Is that what you'd call it? You saw them through a child's eyes. You were fascinated by them…in awe of them because they were so different from—'

'From my mother?' Ruby lifted her chin, a remnant of pride making her spine as straight as a rod. 'Is that what you were going to say?'

The silence throbbed with a dark energy that seemed to press in from all four corners of the room.

Ruby liked to think her mother *had* loved her once. Not that she had any clear memory of it, but still… The alternative was too awful to think about. Didn't most mothers love and adore their babies? Didn't most mothers bond with their newborn infants and want the very best for them?

Or had her mother always resented her? Hated her for changing her life irreparably before she was ready? Resented the demands a small child had made on her time…resented the responsibility that came with raising a child without a father present. Resorted to drugs and drink to escape from the burdensome task of keeping a child safe.

How could Ruby ever know the truth? Her grandmother refused to speak of her daughter—her only child, who had rebelled against everything she had tried to instil in her. The values, the qualities, the solid work ethic...all ignored, disregarded.

And now, of course, it was too late. Ruby's mother had died of an overdose only days after leaving prison, within a year of Ruby coming to live at Rothwell Park.

Lucas finally let out a serrated sigh. 'You deserved better, Ruby. No one can deny that. But my parents were not shining examples of how to be an adult, and certainly not how to be an adult in a relationship.'

Ruby picked up her wine glass again but couldn't bring herself to drink a drop. It was more something to do with her hands. 'But at least they loved you,' she said. She stared at the wine in her glass and added before she could monitor her tongue, 'I'm not sure my mother ever loved me.'

Most people would have said *Of course she did.* Or offered some other equally useless platitude. But not Lucas Rothwell. Maybe there were some advantages to being a hardened cynic. He spoke the blunt truth instead of wrapping it up in cheap shiny tinsel.

'I'm sorry,' he said in a gentle tone. 'That must be hard to live with...not knowing for sure.'

Ruby gave a wry smile, even though she

knew he couldn't see it. She wondered if he would sense it anyway. He seemed to have a sixth sense when it came to her—which, come to think of it, was a scary thought.

Could he sense her growing awareness of him? Could he sense the way her body responded to his closeness? Could he sense how often her gaze drifted to his mouth and how her mind ran wild with images of those firm lips moving against hers?

She put her wine glass back down on the table and ran her fingertip around the rim, so the soft musical whine of the friction filled the silence.

'I couldn't help envying you growing up here at Rothwell Park,' she said, lowering her hand from the glass. 'It's true I was a little starstruck by your parents—in particular your mother. She was so glamorous and vivacious and charming...the life of every party. No wonder your father kept falling in love with her. I think I did a little too.' Ruby gave a little sigh and added, glancing across at him, 'I miss her. I guess you do too.'

Lucas's mouth twisted in a rueful manner, and a shadow of raw grief passed over his features like the ripple of the wind across a lake. 'Yes...' His hand carefully searched for his wine glass and his fingers moved around the stem, but he didn't lift the glass to his lips. 'It's sometimes hard to believe she's gone.' He tapped his fingers on the base of his glass and added with a frown, 'My father certainly got over losing her quickly. He remarried within weeks of her death.'

'But they weren't together at the time,' Ruby pointed out, even though she too had been a bit surprised at Lionel Rothwell's haste in remarrying.

'No, that's true.'

The silence ticked past.

'Do you think they might've got back together? I mean, if she hadn't got sick?' Ruby asked.

'Don't you think three marriages and three divorces is enough to prove two people are completely unsuitable?'

There was a sharp edge to his tone, an embittered edge that was at odds with what Ruby remembered of his parents' relationship. Or maybe he was right—she had been viewing them through the rose-coloured glasses of a love-starved child.

Maybe she was a glass-half-full type of person, but she'd had to live on hope for most of her life. Hope that things would get better…that life would not be uncertain and scary all the time. Hope had helped her build a business with her two best friends. Hope lived in her heart—hope that one day she would find the love of her life and have a happy family.

And her big hope right now was getting Lucas to change his mind about Delphine's wedding before Rothwell Park was sold.

'Lucas… I know you've already said no a thousand times, but please will you consider holding off on the sale of Rothwell Park until after Delphine's wedding? You're selling in any case. What does it matter if a wedding is conducted here in a few weeks' time? It might be the last time I come here. I know it's not really my home, or anything, but I can't help looking upon it as such. It was so wonderful, coming to live here with Gran after a stint in foster care. Please will you think about it some more? I'll stay here for the next week and get the castle tidied up while Gran's in hospital. You won't even know I'm here.'

Lucas let out a long-winded sigh. 'You don't let up, do you?'

'I've learned you don't achieve your goals in life unless you're prepared to work at it.

My credo is: if you've got what it takes, then *do* whatever it takes.'

An enigmatic smile played at the edges of his mouth. She sensed he was mulling something over in his mind. Making calculations that somehow involved her. It gave her a secret thrill to think he might be prepared to cut a deal with her.

'All right, you can hold the wedding here. But I want something in return.'

Ruby's heart did a jerky somersault. 'We're prepared to negotiate on a hiring fee.'

'I'm not talking about money.'

She moistened her parchment-dry lips. 'You're...you're not?'

'I want you to come with me to Greece.'

Ruby stared at him as if he had asked her to go to Mars via Venus. 'But why?'

'Not for the reason you're thinking.'

Her cheeks were so hot she could have fried a couple of eggs on them. 'I wasn't thinking any such thing.'

His smile tilted a little higher on one side. 'I'll organise the cleaning of Rothwell Park while we're away. If I'm not on site it will lessen the chance of a press leak. We'll stay for a week on my private island and—'

Ruby's eyes threatened to pop right out of her head. 'You have a *private island*?'

'I bought it a few months ago—before I was diagnosed with the tumour. It's undergone some extensive renovations since, but I haven't seen the finished result. I have to do a final inspection for the builder.'

'But you can't see anything other than vague shapes and light and dark, right?'

'True, but I can use my other senses. Anyway, you can be my eyes. You can describe everything to me in intricate detail. But it goes without saying that if you betray me to the press the wedding is off, understood?'

'I would never do something like that.'

'I'll organise someone to visit your grandmother at the hospital,' Lucas said. 'She has a couple of friends she plays bridge with occasionally who'll look in on her, so you won't need to worry about her while we're away.'

While we're away...

A frisson passed over Ruby's flesh at how strangely intimate those words sounded. She would be alone with Lucas Rothwell on his private island for a week. A hot tingle rolled down the length of her spine. She would be by his side, talking him through what she saw.

But what if he sensed her heightened awareness of him? What if she was tempted to touch him again? He was a magnet to her iron—a potent, powerful force she was drawn to almost against her will. Almost, because a secret part of her still felt cheated that she had never got to experience the firm, sensual press of his lips on hers.

'But what will I say to Aerin and Harper? They only expected me to be away for the weekend. I'll have to tell them something...' She bit down on her lower lip, not sure she liked the thought of lying to her friends—especially Harper, who had been lied to all her life.

'Tell them you're doing me a favour in order to secure Rothwell Park.'

'They'll think I'm having a fling with you.'

One dark eyebrow lifted. 'Would they disapprove if you were?'

Ruby shrugged. 'Maybe... Especially Harper. I told her a few months back to steer clear of a notorious playboy at a wedding we were doing. But Jack Livingstone was not so easy for her to ignore.'

He jerked upright in his chair like a

puppet whose strings had been suddenly tugged. 'Jack Livingstone, the boutique hotelier?' His expression was quickly smoothed over, as if he was conscious of his reaction and wanted to downplay it. 'What happened?' His tone had switched to mild interest, as if he were making polite conversation rather than avidly searching for details.

'He was the best man, and in a moment of weakness she had a one-night stand with him. He wanted to see her again, but she wouldn't return his calls.'

'Why not?'

'He's a playboy and she thinks he only wants to see her again because she's the first woman who's ever said no to him.'

Lucas twisted his mouth as if he understood all too well the way a playboy's mind worked. 'A challenge can be hard to resist.' He picked up his wine glass. 'So, will you come with me?'

A flutter of excitement danced across the floor of her belly. 'How can I say no?'

Later that night Lucas sat in the library, sipping a nightcap on his own, mulling over his decision to take Ruby with him to his island. He wasn't a man to make impulsive decisions, but it made sense to invite her rather than anyone else. Besides, he couldn't bear to be at Rothwell Park while the place was being cleaned from top to bottom.

It would be too risky being there while strangers came in to clean. Strangers who might purposely or inadvertently let something slip to the press or on social media. Of course, rather than take Ruby to Greece he could have paid someone to accompany him—a member of staff, perhaps. But spending a week on his island with a staff member did not appeal to him half as much as a week with Ruby did.

A week alone with Ruby.

A warning bell sounded in his subconscious, but he blocked it out with logical argument. Ruby wanted something from him and he would give it to her if she upheld her end of the deal. She had too much at stake to betray his trust. He realised with a strange little jolt that he did trust her. She wanted this celebrity wedding to go ahead so she could build her business. He admired her goal-driven focus for it reminded him of his own. Success did not come about by wishing for it. You had to work for it— sometimes doing things you would rather not do.

But he didn't get the sense that Ruby found the prospect of a week in his company on his island all that distasteful. Interesting… Did that mean she hadn't outgrown her crush? She was no longer an awkward teenager. She was a fully grown woman. An intriguing and captivating young woman he found increasingly impossible to ignore.

From the moment Ruby had walked into the library something had changed for him. Something had changed *in* him. Her touch had ignited a spark inside him—lit a fuse that was fizzing quietly but insistently in his veins even now. One might argue that he was being reckless in taking her with him to his island. But something about her made him feel more alive than he had felt in weeks—months, even.

She wasn't the type of woman to kowtow to him. She stood her ground and fought from her corner and argued her case with steely determination. She was passionate and feisty and, God, how he needed someone to make him feel something other than this quiet despair at being at Rothwell Park when he could be on his beautiful island in the sun.

This actor's wedding could be the farewell event before Lucas left Rothwell Park for good. He had no emotional attachment to the place—to him it represented pain and broken promises and shattered hopes.

He would be relieved to drive out through the gate for a final time.

'You're going *where*?' Harper said on another three-way phone call later that night.

'It's only for a week, and it's the only way I can get Lucas to agree to have Delphine's wedding here at Rothwell Park,' Ruby said.

'Why does he want you to go with him?' Aerin asked with a hint of delighted suspicion in her tone. 'What's going on between you two?'

'Nothing.' Ruby was glad it wasn't a video call, because right now her cheeks were glowing hot enough to blowtorch the sugar on the top of a crème brûlée. 'He wants me to see his newly renovated villa. I thought I might as well go and check it out. I haven't had a holiday in ages, and I happen to be free this week.'

'Playboys aren't worth the trouble,' Harper said. 'Take it from someone who knows about these things.'

'Aren't you being a little hard on Jack?' Ruby said. 'He did want to see you again, but you point-blank refused.'

'Hey, you were the one who warned me about him in the first place.'

'I know—but he asked to see you again, so you must have made an impression on him,' Ruby said.

'I'm not ready for a relationship—not even a fling,' Harper said. 'Work is my focus right now. I shouldn't have allowed him to distract me at the Tenterbury wedding. It was unprofessional of me, and it's all the more reason for me to stay away from him.'

'Well, *I'm* ready for a relationship,' Aerin said with wistful sigh. 'The trouble is finding Mr Right when there are so many Mr Wrongs out there.'

'Don't you mean Mr Perfect?' Ruby said with a teasing note to her voice.

At nearly thirty, Aerin was still a virgin. In fact, she was so terrified of dating the wrong man she hadn't even been kissed.

'Paint me overly cautious, but I don't want a trail of broken relationships behind me before I find my soulmate,' Aerin said. 'I want what my parents and siblings have—true and lasting love with a partner who's perfect for them.'

'Don't we all?' Ruby sighed.

'Which is why I have serious misgivings

about you spending a week with a renowned playboy on a private island,' Harper said. 'You had a crush on him before. It wouldn't take much for you to develop one again.'

'Stop worrying about me,' Ruby said. 'I can take care of myself.'

Now all she had to do was prove it.

CHAPTER FOUR

THE FLIGHT TO Athens was uneventful, especially since Lucas had organised a private jet. While they were waiting for their transfer Ruby took the opportunity to buy a swimsuit and a sarong, and other essential items, given she only had her weekend clothes with her. None of which were suitable for a Greek island.

She went back to where Lucas was waiting for her in a private lounge area.

'Did you get everything you need?'

'I think so. How soon do we board the next plane?'

'Not a plane. A helicopter. Stavros, the pilot, is waiting for us now.'

A cold hand of fear gripped at her insides, squeezing, twisting, torturing. She looked out of the window to where a helicopter was stationed. *A helicopter?* Even saying the word in her mind was enough to send her spiralling into panic. Seeing those powerful blades reminded her of a flight when she was a young child, with one of her mother's boyfriends. The boyfriend had seemed to enjoy her terror, and had shredded her tender nerves with his reckless behaviour as pilot.

She hadn't been in a helicopter since. She'd been lucky in her career so far and had not needed to fly in one, but with the growing popularity of destination weddings she knew it wouldn't be long before she would have to face down her fear.

'Can't we go by boat?' Ruby asked.

'It's quicker by air.'

She shifted her weight from foot to foot, glancing with trepidation at the helicopter waiting on the tarmac in the bright, shimmering sunshine. 'B-but it'd be nice going by boat. The fresh air, the scenery—we might even see dolphins.'

Lucas turned his head in her direction and frowned in concern. 'Are you scared of helicopters?'

His tone was gentle, not the least bit mocking, and it made it so much harder to maintain her emotional distance. Ruby moistened her suddenly dry lips, conscious of how close he was standing to her. His rolled-up shirtsleeve brushed against the bare skin of her arm and an electrifying tingle raced along her flesh and tripped her pulse.

'A little…'

'Have you had a bad experience in one?'

Even though she knew he couldn't see her expression, she sensed he could read her distress signals. Her rapid breathing, her racing pulse, her agitated movements. He could probably even hear her churning stomach.

'When I was seven my mother had a rich boyfriend who had a helicopter pilot's licence. He was also a drug dealer.' She glanced at the helicopter again and shuddered. 'He got a kick out of seeing how frightened I was when he made dangerous moves.' She swallowed and added, 'I haven't been in one since…'

Lucas placed a stabilising hand on her shoulder. 'What a cruel thing to do to a small, sensitive child.' His voice was throbbing with barely suppressed anger on her behalf. 'Didn't your mother tell him to stop?'

'No, she thought it was funny. She liked the daredevil lifestyle he offered and thought I needed to be toughened up.' She twisted her lips and added, 'She blamed me when they broke up a few weeks later. She said he couldn't cope with a kid who still wet the bed at seven years old.'

'Oh, Ruby…'

Lucas gathered her in his arms, resting his chin on the top of her head. His arms were strong and yet infinitely gentle, as if he was reaching back through time to comfort that small, terrified little girl.

Ruby breathed in the scent of him—the citrus top notes of his aftershave with its hints of wood and leather. Her face was pressed against the freshly laundered cotton of his shirt, which was the only barrier between her skin and the toned muscles of his chest. She could feel the steady *tump-tump-tump* of his heart against her cheek and her own heart went into a hit-and-miss rhythm, along with her pulse. She became aware of how close her lower body was to his. Her soft contours moulded against his hard frame, stirring her feminine flesh, igniting needs she fought desperately to control.

Lucas gently put her from him, but kept his hands on the tops of her shoulders. The only sign that he might be as rattled by her closeness as she was by his was a dull flush riding high along his aristocratic cheekbones.

'Hey, you'll be fine with me. I've flown heaps of times and never had an incident. I would fly us myself, except for my current condition.'

'You have a helicopter licence?'

He gave a grim movement of his mouth that loosely passed for a rueful smile and his hands fell away from her shoulders, one of them raking through his hair. 'Yes—not that it's much use to me at present.'

Ruby placed her fingers on the bare hair-roughened skin of his tanned wrist. Another lightning zap of electricity shot up her arm, and she knew he must have felt a similar reaction for he gave a tiny flinch, but didn't move his wrist away from her touch.

'It must be difficult to not know if you will regain your full vision.'

Lucas placed his hand over hers, anchoring it to the strong warmth of his wrist. His expression was difficult to read, given he was wearing his aviator glasses. 'We can take a boat if you can't face flying in the helicopter. But I have engaged a pilot with a lot of experience, and I'll be by your side the whole time.'

Ruby knew he wanted to get to his island as soon as he could, and she was touched that he was prepared to put her concerns ahead of his own. She glanced down at their joined hands and suppressed a tiny shiver. Not of fear but of excitement. His skin was deeply tanned, and the rough, masculine hair sprinkled on his arm and over the back of his hand was a heady reminder of the powerful male hormones charging through his body. The hormones that were signalling to her female ones and sending them a little haywire.

She took a shaky breath and slipped her hand out of his hold. 'It's okay. I'll be brave. I might get seasick otherwise—and that could be infinitely worse.'

His sudden smile transformed his features, making him appear younger and more approachable. And even more dangerously irresistible.

Lucas held Ruby's small hand in his once they'd taken their seats in the four-person helicopter. He could feel the tremor of her fingers and gave them a reassuring squeeze.

Touching her had become rather a habit— a habit he found increasingly hard to resist. Holding her in his arms had made his blood tingle as it had never tingled before. Her body was slim and utterly feminine, each soft curve stirring his body into rampant lust. Perhaps it was his current sex drought, or perhaps it was because he couldn't see but could only feel. All he knew was that he had to be careful around her. She was not his type and he wasn't hers. A fling between them would be completely inadvisable...even if it was sorely tempting.

Lucas was still brooding with anger over how she had been treated in her early childhood. The cruelty was unpardonable, and all these years later Ruby was clearly still carrying the scars. It was ironic that she'd found coming to live on his family estate so stabilising, for he had never experienced it as anything but a battleground for overblown egos. But, putting his parents' issues aside, Ruby had benefited from living there with her grandmother.

He could understand why she would be upset about him selling Rothwell Park. And she would potentially be even more upset when she found out who was buying it. She had already mentioned the hotel billionaire Jack Livingstone in regard to her friend Harper. Lucas should have told her then and there that Jack was the buyer, but he and Jack had signed an agreement to keep the details confidential until the sale was finalised.

The pilot started the engine and Ruby flinched as the rotor blades began to spin. Lucas lifted her hand and laid it on his thigh, speaking to her through the headset microphone. 'Breathe, Ruby...nice and deep and slow. Exhale on the count of three...let go of all your tension with each breath out.'

She dug her nails into his thigh, as if anchoring herself to him. He couldn't hear above the noise of the engine or through the headset whether her breathing had slowed once the helicopter rose in the air, but gradually her grip on his thigh relaxed.

'Are we up very high? I'm not brave enough to open my eyes yet.'

'And here I was, relying on you to tell me what you see.' He kept his tone light.

Ruby's hand slipped off his thigh and he had to stop himself from reaching for it to bring it back. He sensed her shifting in her seat to look out of the window at her side.

'The water is so blue.'

'What shade of blue?'

'A gorgeous turquoise that makes you want to dive in and swim for hours...'

Her voice took on a dreamy note and he pictured her swimming like a mermaid in the ocean.

'What else do you see?'

'A few white clouds.'

'What type of clouds?'

'Hey, I was never that good at geography. Clouds are just clouds to me.'

Lucas gave a wry smile. 'Are they high or low?'

'High and kind of thready—like stretched out cotton wool.'

'They would be cirrus clouds.'

'Oh, right.' She leaned closer to her window. 'Oh, my goodness. I think I can see dolphins. A whole pod of them. Wow!'

'Describe them to me.'

'There's about ten or so, and they're all swimming in one direction—perhaps feeding on a school of fish. The water on their backs as they breach to take in air shines like millions of diamonds. They're so sleek and nimble, so fluid in the water...'

The breathless wonder in her voice entranced him so much that he could picture what she described in his mind.

'Oh, wow, one has just leapt out of the water and splashed back down. The sun caught his silver back and dorsal fin. I've never seen anything so incredibly beautiful...'

Lucas wished he could see the awe on her face, but he realised that listening to her had its own reward. 'What else can you see?'

'Erm… Oh, there's a boat—well, I guess you'd call it a yacht if you want to get all technical. A luxury yacht. It's white, with a blue and silver trim, and it looks like you could sleep ten people or more on board. And to the west is what looks like a couple of fishing boats.'

'We should be getting close to my island now.'

'Already?'

'I can hear Stavros preparing to descend.'

Ruby put her hand back on his thigh. 'Thank you.'

'For?'

'For making me forget about how terrified I was.'

Lucas could make out the vague shape of her face and lifted his hand to stroke two of his fingers down the slope of her cheek. It was like the finest silk under his fingertips, and he wished he could touch more of her. *All* of her.

'You did extremely well.'

His voice came out sandpaper-rough. He heard the sound of her breath, felt the soft waft of it against his face. She gave an audible swallow and his nostrils flared as her flowery fragrance teased his senses into a drugged stupor. Never had he wanted to kiss a woman more than at this moment. Desire roared in his blood, thundered in his pulse, thickened his male flesh to the point of pain.

He cradled one side of her face, his thumb stroking the rounded curve of her small chin. 'You have incredibly soft skin.'

One of her hands came up to the side of his face, and she moved her fingers across the thick growth of stubble. 'You need a shave.'

Her voice was lightly teasing, but there was a quality to it that spoke to the dark desires swirling in his body. Dark and forbidden desires that threatened to break free of the tight restraints he had around them. He could feel them tugging on the cords of his self-control like a wild animal, fighting, raging, desperately clawing for freedom.

'Are you worried about getting beard rash?' Lucas kept his tone light-hearted, but his intention was deadly serious. He longed to feel the softness of her lips against his. Longed for it like a potent drug.

'I would be…if you kissed me.'

Her voice was as husky as his had been just moments earlier. Lucas ran his thumb across the plump shape of her lower lip, re-calling its sweet contour in his mind. 'I'm not sure that would be such a good idea right now...'

'Oh?'

There was a wealth of disappointment in her one-word response.

He gave a rueful twist of his mouth and removed his hand from her face. 'I wouldn't want to shock Stavros.'

'Because seeing you kiss the house-keeper's granddaughter *would* be shock-ing, right?'

On the surface her tone was as light-hearted as his, but underneath he could hear a trace of wounded pride.

Lucas took off his headset and hung it over the back of the pilot's seat in front of him. 'That would depend on the type of kiss.'

He could almost sense her frowning at him. 'How would you kiss me? I mean, hypothetically speaking, if we *were* to kiss.'

'That would depend on where we were.' He sent a playful smile her way and added, 'If we were in company, then a light peck on the cheek. But if we were alone...'

He left the rest of the sentence hanging, wishing he could see the expression on her face. He didn't want to question why he was flirting with her. He was enjoying their banter way too much. Enjoying the thought of actually kissing her, moving his mouth against the softness of hers and letting things go from there... His body thickened in anticipation, the turgid heat of his arousal reminding him of the fine line he was walking.

A dangerous line.

A line he had promised he would never walk near, let alone cross.

'But we're going to be alone,' Ruby said. 'For a week. Or do you have staff on the island?'

'Yes and no. There's a maintenance man and his wife who look after the house. Their quarters are on the other side of the island, but they're away at present, visiting their adult children on Santorini. I asked them to organise food and supplies, and for the beds to be made up in the villa, but for the rest of the time we'll be alone until Stavros comes to take us back to Athens.'

Ruby unclipped her seat belt. 'You really

are serious about maintaining your privacy, aren't you?'

'You bet I am.'

Maybe he should have organised a chaperon. Maybe he shouldn't have brought Ruby here in the first place. Maybe he needed to get a grip and take their relationship back to what it had been before—distant, formal. But something had shifted in the last twenty-four hours. Something that couldn't be so easily dialled back. There was a new sense of intimacy, a sharing of hurts and wounds from the past that had somehow breached the chasm that had existed between them before.

And being so far away from Rothwell Park added another dimension to their relationship. Being away from his ancestral home always gave him a sense of freedom, a sense of living in the moment rather than in the past. But was living in the moment with Ruby a good idea or a bad idea?

All he knew was that he trusted her to help him sign off on the inspection of the villa for the builder. Her attention to detail was similar to his own—little escaped her. Would she notice the way he was drawn to her, even though everything rational and logical in his mind told him to keep his distance?

He had made it a whole lot harder to keep his distance by bringing her to his island.

They would be totally alone.

CHAPTER FIVE

A FEW MINUTES LATER, Ruby stepped down from the helicopter on legs that were not quite steady—not because of the flight, but because of how close she had come to leaning closer and kissing Lucas.

The temptation to do so had been close to overwhelming. She had forgotten all about the pilot, forgotten all about the dreaded flight—all she had been focussed on was Lucas. In the space of a few hours he had become her entire focus. She was aware of him in a way she hadn't been before. Aware of the magnetic pull of his body to her sensually starved one. Aware of the subtle change in their relationship that was not just about his current blindness but something else—something she couldn't quite describe.

What had she got herself into by coming with him to his private island? Normally she was so straight down the line and sensible. She wasn't the type to do things on a whim, to be impulsive or reckless. But it seemed there was a secret part of her that was all those things—or at least when she was with Lucas Rothwell.

She was starting to understand why Harper had found it so hard to resist Jack Livingstone. What was it about renowned playboys that was so darn irresistible? Not that Ruby had ever considered Lucas a particularly charming man. He had always been so brusque and aloof with her in the past. But his gentle handling of her phobic reaction to the helicopter flight had revealed a tender and compassionate side to his personality that was equally addictive as full-blown charm. Perhaps even more so.

Ruby stood for a moment, taking in her surroundings. The island was larger than she had been expecting, with a forest of cypress pines behind the helicopter landing spot. It was fringed by sandy beaches, one of which had a jetty near a luxury villa.

She lifted her face to the sun to breathe in the salty sea air. 'I feel like I've stepped into a fairy tale.'

'It's a nice place. Serene, peaceful...'

'I love serene and peaceful,' Ruby said,

linking her arm through his as they followed Stavros, who was taking their luggage on ahead. 'I used to dream of visiting a place like this when I was a kid. You should've seen some of the places I lived in before I came to live with Gran. It would have made your skin crawl.'

'I hate the thought of you suffering like that.' His voice was laced with anger. 'Some people don't deserve to have children.'

'Careful, there's a couple of steps here on the path,' Ruby said. 'I'm just glad I had Gran and your parents. They were kind to me—especially your mother. I remember once she let me play dress-up with some of her clothes and jewellery. I had the best fun. I pretended I was a movie star. She even gave me a bright red lipstick to use. Gran took it off me, of course. She's not a make-up person.'

Lucas stopped walking to look in the direction of the cypress forest, his brow furrowed in a frown. 'My mother lost a baby before I was born. It was a little girl. They—or I should say Mum—called her Sophia. My father was against naming a miscarried child.'

Ruby's heart contracted. 'I didn't know that. How terribly sad.'

Lucas continued walking along the path with her. 'Yes, I imagine it was. I don't think my father is the type of man to understand how a woman would feel about such things. He refused to talk about it—ever. It was as if it had never happened. My mother was thrilled when she got pregnant with me, but I've always wondered if she was disappointed that she didn't have another little girl to replace the one she lost.'

This time it was Ruby who stopped walking to look up at him. 'But she loved you, Lucas. You're surely not in doubt of that?'

He gave a loose shrug of one broad shoulder, his lips set in a grim line. 'It was a difficult birth, and she had a long bout of postnatal depression afterwards. A nanny was engaged for me, and she ended up staying on until I went to boarding school at six. My mother loved me in her way, but she never stopped grieving for the child she lost. Unfortunately, due to the complications of my birth, there was no possibility of her having any more children.'

'No wonder your parents had such a rocky relationship,' Ruby said. 'There were so many unresolved issues. But I wonder why Gran didn't tell me any of this.'

'Your grandmother is an old-school

housekeeper. What goes on up upstairs, stays upstairs.'

Ruby wondered what her gran would think of her spending a week alone with Lucas Rothwell. When she had quickly visited her in hospital, before leaving, she had been a little sketchy on the details, simply saying she was filling in for her as housekeeper.

She resumed walking with Lucas up the path leading to the villa. 'I'm sorry I didn't know more about your mother's pain. I might've been able to comfort her in some way.'

'You did comfort her,' Lucas said with heavy conviction. 'She loved it when you came to live at Rothwell. She would be so proud of you now...to see how you've turned out. A smart and successful businesswoman who sets goals and works hard to achieve them, no matter what obstacles are in her way.'

'*You've* been my biggest obstacle so far.' Ruby gave him a playful shoulder-bump. 'Go on—admit it.'

He made a soft sound of wry amusement. 'But you won me over in the end.'

Ruby wasn't so sure about that...

They said their goodbyes to Stavros and he went back to the helicopter. Within a few minutes Ruby watched it take off and rise into the sky, and finally disappear in the distance. This was it—she was finally alone with Lucas. On a private island, no less.

The newly constructed villa was set on a freshly landscaped area a few hundred metres from the main beach. Ruby shielded her eyes from the blinding sunlight and looked critically at the design. She was no architect, but it was impossible to find fault with it.

The lines were modern and minimalist, a pavilion-style design, and it was built on one level. The front of the villa overlooked a large infinity pool that was only a few steps from the main living area. The use of local stone made the villa blend perfectly into the setting. And, while the garden was still in its infancy, the same stone had been used in the terraced areas, softened by lush greenery here and there.

It was quite easily the most luxurious setting she had ever seen, and the thought that Lucas could not see it and might never do so was particularly poignant.

'It's gorgeous, Lucas. Did you design it yourself?'

'Yes—with a bit of help from a friend who's a building architect.'

'It's a beautiful setting with the forest behind. I can smell the pines from here. And don't get me started about the pool... I don't think I've ever seen a more inviting one.'

'I'm glad you like it.' He reached down to brush his hand against one of the newly planted shrubs near the front entrance. 'These will grow in time. It'll take a year or two to get the garden the way I want it. But gardening is always about patience.'

'I like how you've made the villa blend into the landscape. A lot of modern buildings can look a little out of place, but not this one. I can't wait to see inside.'

Lucas waved a hand in the direction of the entrance. 'Come this way. Stavros has opened up and taken our luggage inside. Let's have a cool drink and then you can have a look around.'

'Sounds like a plan.'

Ruby walked with him inside the front entrance of the villa. The floor inside was of stunning polished marble, in cream and beige tones that reminded her of sand patterns on the shoreline. The view from the full-length windows was spectacular, as beyond the of the pool it faced the stunning blue of the ocean with its fringe of powder-white sand. The interior walls were painted a chalk-white, and to balance it, the light fittings were in a modern minimalist style and matte black. The furniture was also modern and streamlined, but there were classical touches here and there that gave the villa a lovely balance of old and new, adding a depth of character than a brand-new home often lacked.

Ruby let out a breath of awe. 'Oh, my goodness, it's so beautiful...'

A smile curved his mouth and her heart gave a little flick-kick. He was so devastatingly attractive when he smiled. It relaxed his sternly cast features and made him seem more approachable.

'The kitchen is through there.' He pointed to the right of the living area that overlooked the pool. 'I'd offer to help, but—'

'Don't be silly—it's what I'm here for. Why don't you wait on the terrace for me? Do you need help getting out there?'

'No.' A note of pride entered his tone and his features tightened into a brooding frown. 'I think I can manage not to tumble into the pool.'

'I'm sorry...' She bit her lip. 'I didn't mean to—'

'Don't apologise.' He released a short gust of air and twisted his mouth in a rueful line, the harsh lines on his face relaxing slightly. 'I guess I didn't expect to be here for the first time after the build under these circumstances.'

'It must be horrendously frustrating for you.'

'It more ways than the obvious.'

The enigmatic quality to his words made her skin tingle. Was he referring to their almost-kiss on the helicopter?

Ruby found the kitchen and set about organising some refreshments from the supplies his staff had delivered. Within a few minutes she had tall glasses of fresh juice and a fruit and cheese platter on a tray. She carried it out to where Lucas was sitting on one of two sun lounger chairs next to the pool. The roof of the villa jutted out over them, to bring much-needed shade to the sun-drenched terrace.

Ever the well-bred gentleman, he rose when he heard her approach. 'Did you find everything all right?'

'Yes—there's no shortage of food or drink, that's for sure. Here we go.' Ruby set the tray on the table between the two loungers and then handed him a glass of juice.

'Thank you.' He waited until she took her

seat before he sat in his. Then he crossed one muscled leg over his bent knee and lifted his glass to his lips.

Ruby found it hard not to stare at him, taking in every one of his features—the way his lips moved against the rim of the glass, the way the strong column of his throat moved up and down as he swallowed, the way his long, tanned fingers held the frosted glass… It made her wonder how it would feel to have those fingers touching her intimately.

Her inner core tightened, moistened, pulsed with a clawing longing, and she crossed her legs to try and suppress the wayward desires.

'Tell me what you can see right now.'

Lucas's deep voice jolted her out of her study of him.

'Erm… I was actually looking at you.'

One side of his mouth lifted at the corner. 'And what do you see?'

She licked her dry lips and put her glass down on the table between them, the shade and the light sea breeze doing little to cool the heat in her cheeks. 'You seem a little more relaxed now you're here. You've even smiled, which you don't often do.'

A frown carved into his forehead. 'You

find that a fault? That I don't find life all that amusing at present?'

'It's understandable that you'd be feeling frustrated and annoyed at losing your eyesight. I can only imagine how hard it must be.'

'Close your eyes and imagine it now. Go on. Sit with me here and experience it like I do.'

'Okay...'

Ruby closed her eyes and listened to the sound of the birds twittering in the nearby shrubbery. The sound of the gentle lapping of the ocean in the distance was soothing, mesmerising, and even the light dance of the breeze amongst the leaves of the shrubbery had a calming effect on her senses.

'It's amazing what you can hear when you can only hear and not see. It's like every sound is magnified.'

'Keep your eyes closed and come over to me. Don't cheat. Find your way by touch.'

Ruby found herself taking up his challenge, wanting to prove to him that she was prepared to put herself in his situation in order to better understand his experience of the world at this point. She had an advantage, though, because she had already seen the table between them, and the general layout of the terrace and the dimensions of the pool.

She walked with slow, cautious steps towards him, sidestepping the table and coming to within touching distance of his legs.

'Now take my glass off me and put it on the table.'

Ruby reached out her hand and finally located the glass in his hand, briefly encountering his fingers as she took it from him. She half turned and placed it on the table behind her, making sure first that the surface was clear and the glass would be not too close to the edge. The amount of concentration it took was a revelation to her, and the dangers of breaking a glass or misjudging where a piece of hard furniture might be placed only added to the stress.

'Gosh, this is a lot harder than I thought.'

'Take my hand.'

His voice had a note of command to it that was strangely compelling. Ruby kept her eyes closed and searched for his hand, finally finding it resting on his thigh.

She curled her fingers around his and lifted his hand. 'Now what?'

Lucas rose in one agile movement, standing so close to her she could feel his knees against hers. 'Are your eyes still closed?'

His tone had a husky edge that sent a shiver racing down her spine.

'Yes...' Her voice was as whisper-soft as the breeze teasing the leaves of the shrubbery.

Her heart beat a staccato rhythm that made her feel light-headed and unsteady on her feet. She could feel herself swaying towards him, the magnetic pull of his male body calling out to everything that was female in hers. It was an irresistible forcefield of longing that made a mockery of her determination to keep her distance.

One of his hands cupped the left side of her face, his fingers splaying across her cheek. Tingling sensations rippled through her body and spot fires of need burned in her female flesh. His other hand tipped up her chin, his thumbpad stroking over the fullness of her lower lip.

'You have a beautiful mouth.'

His tone was still pitched low and deep, with a rough edge that set her pulse racing all over again.

'But you can't see it...or at least not clearly.' Ruby couldn't get her voice above a thready whisper, or her heartrate to settle into a more normal rhythm.

'But I can feel it.'

She snatched in a wobbly breath, her heart skipping all over the place. 'What does it feel like?'

'Soft, sensual, sexy...'

His voice went down even lower, to a deep rumbling burr that made heat flow down her spine like warmed honey.

'I don't think anyone has ever used those three words in relation to me before.'

'I find that hard to believe.'

There was a beat or two of silence. A silence that had an anticipatory element, like a long-held breath while someone waited for an important announcement.

Lucas brushed his fingertips over her closed eyelids. 'I thought you would've peeked by now.'

'I'm tempted.'

'So am I.'

Something about the cryptic quality of his tone sent another shiver rolling down her spin. Then he cradled her face in both of his hands, his touch light and yet possessive.

'Are you asking me to kiss you?'

'I'm not asking you to do anything you don't want to do.'

Ruby slipped her arms around his waist, abandoning her pride in her quest to feel his mouth on hers, emboldened by the feeling sweeping through her body. The desire licking along her veins was sending heat to all of her erogenous zones. A blistering heat that made her aware of every inch of her flesh—especially where it was in contact with his.

Lucas brought his mouth down to hers in a kiss that was as soft as the landing of a breeze-blown leaf. He lifted it off, but then came back down with greater pressure, his lips moving against hers in a sensual manner that sent every female hormone in her body into a happy dance. He made a sound deep in his throat...a guttural sound that was as primal as an animal growl... and then he deepened the kiss with a commanding thrust of his tongue.

Ruby opened to him with a gasp of delight, her legs almost going from beneath her as desire hit her like a tidal wave. His tongue danced and duelled with hers, teasing her senses into overdrive. His hands were still cradling her face, his lips locked on hers, and their bodies were close enough for her to feel every deliciously hard ridge of his.

His lips moved with greater urgency against hers, his tongue playing cat-and-mouse with hers in darting thrusts that sent heat flowing to her core like molten lava. He shifted position, letting his hands fall away from her face to gather her closer by grasping her by the hips. She gasped at the intimate contact with his bold erection, wanting him with a need that was unlike anything she had experienced in the past.

Lucas suddenly broke the kiss with a muttered curse, releasing his hold on her. He pushed his hair back from his face with a rough hand that didn't appear too steady.

'I didn't bring you here to seduce you.'

There was anger in his voice, but she sensed it was directed at himself, not her.

Ruby licked her lips and tasted the sexy salt of his kiss. 'I know.' She smothered her disappointment behind an airy, light-hearted tone. 'You and me, right? Like *that* could ever work.' She moved away to pick up her fruit juice, adding, 'I'm going to have a little scout around before I make dinner. Is there anything I can get you in the meantime?'

'No.' His lips were set in a grim line and he added after a stiffly released breath, 'Thank you.'

She had only taken half a dozen steps when his voice stopped her in her tracks. 'Ruby?'

Ruby turned to look at him. 'Yes?'

He released a long, jagged breath, his expression as hard and impenetrable as the stonework beneath his feet. 'It won't happen again.'

It must not happen again, Lucas determined once Ruby's footsteps had faded into the distance.

He was furious with himself for giving in to a moment of weakness—a moment of sensual madness that could only backfire if he allowed it free rein. He could still taste her on his lips...the sweet milk and honey taste that had made his senses spin out of control. He was wary of allowing any dalliance between them. Not because of their history per se, but because he wasn't the knight in shining armour she was looking for.

But it didn't mean he didn't want her.

He did. Damnably so.

But just because he wanted something it didn't mean he could have it. He of all people should know that by now.

Like most people, he had taken his sight for granted, never once dreaming it might be taken from him—even temporarily. His career had been built around his ability to see. The career he loved and had worked so hard to build to this point was hanging by the hope that his sight would be restored. He couldn't envisage continuing as a landscape architect without his vision. Nor could he bear the thought of his condition being media fodder—yet another Rothwell scandal to sell newspapers and gossip magazines. His parents' behaviour throughout his life had put a target on his back. Anything he did, anywhere he went, anyone he associated with drew the press to him like bees to pollen.

This week on his private island was meant to be a way for him to get away from Rothwell Park while it was being cleaned in preparation for Delphine Rainbird's wedding. To rest, to recuperate, to regroup. Not to indulge in a fling with Ruby Pennington…even if the desire to do so was burning a hole in the armour of his self-control like a blowtorch on butter.

Lucas lifted his face to the sun, smelled the spicy scent of the cypress pines behind the villa redolent in the air. He had only been to the island once before he'd bought it several months ago. He had been too busy juggling various large projects across the globe. How ironic that now he finally had the time to be here he couldn't see a damn thing other than vague shapes. He was a details guy—a perfectionist who prided himself on delivering a high standard on every task he set himself.

He knew many blind people lived happy and fulfilling lives, but he couldn't get his head around being one of them.

He *wanted* his sight back.

He *grieved* for the ability to see.

He *mourned* the loss of little things, like not being able to see the sunset, the sunrise, the smile on someone's face…

Yes, he could manage to dress and feed himself, and he could mostly manage to avoid bumping into furniture, but what he wanted was his old life back. The freedom to come and go, the independence, the autonomy, the agency. He was stuck in a foreign land, on unfamiliar territory, where all he could cling to was a thread of hope that his life would go back to how it had been before.

And he didn't need his sight to recognise that he had seriously miscalculated how tempting it would be to have Ruby here with him. What had he been thinking, getting her to close her eyes and pretend to be blind? It had only intensified the sensual atmosphere between them. The bewitching atmosphere that had grown from the moment she'd stepped into the library at Rothwell Park and asked him about the wedding.

He could have stuck to his refusal. He could have been stubborn and unbending. But he hadn't wanted to jeopardise her business aspirations. In some ways she reminded him of himself—hardworking, driven, determined. It hadn't sat well with him to thwart her plan. He was selling Rothwell Park anyway. What did it matter if one wedding was held there before he handed over the deeds?

Lucas only hoped his determination to keep his hands off Ruby held out over the next seven days, otherwise he was in deep trouble.

Deeper than he wanted to think about.

CHAPTER SIX

RUBY FOUND THE rooms that had been prepared for her by Lucas's housekeeper. The
bedroom was larger than her entire flat
back in London, decorated in cream and
white, with a luxurious handwoven rug on
the floor that threatened to swallow her up
to the waist. And the bathroom was stun-
ningly appointed, with the same sand-in-
spired marble floor and tapware in gold.

The shower area was big enough to have
a party in, and there was a deep freestand-
ing bath positioned in front of a window
that overlooked a secluded walled garden.
A young vine was beginning its climb
along the stonework outside, and a bronze
fountain with a tinkling flow of water gave
the setting a spa-like feel. The large pavilion-style windows of the bedroom had a
stunning view of the ocean, to the left of
the jetty.

She opened the sliding glass doors leading to the terrace and the briny scent of the ocean filled her nostrils. The lightweight silk curtains, captured by the playful sea breeze, billowed around her and out through the doors like the voluminous skirt of a ballgown.

Ruby caught sight of Lucas, down by the water's edge. He was standing with his back to the villa, his hand thrust deeply into his trouser pockets. Was he still deriding himself for kissing her? The housekeeper's granddaughter who had, yet again, made a fool of herself over him? But he had been the one to start it by insisting she close her eyes and try to see the world from his perspective.

Ruby ran her tongue over her lips and recalled every moment of their heart-stopping kiss. No one had ever kissed her with such intensity, with such exquisite sensuality. He had stirred her body into a swarm of sensations it was still humming with even now.

Lucas turned and faced the villa, and even though Ruby knew he couldn't see her she suspected he sensed her watching him. But how could she *not* watch him? Not be transfixed by him? Captivated by him? He had always held a certain fascination for her—her teenage crush was a cringeworthy reminder of that—and in her callow youth she had elevated him to a godlike status, finding him a powerfully romantic figure: a tortured hero who only needed the love of the right woman to find peace.

Ruby had gauchely, misguidedly, imagined herself as that woman, foolishly thinking she was his perfect soul mate. But he didn't even believe such a thing existed. He was as cynical about relationships as she was hopeful and optimistic. One kiss did not mean anything, and she had better hammer that truth into her brain right now or suffer the humiliating consequences of having her hopes dashed all over again.

Ruby had spent an hour in the dream of a kitchen, preparing dinner. Cinderella had never had it so good. The appliances were top-of-the-range, and the layout was perfect in terms of form and function. She couldn't have designed it better herself.

She hadn't seen Lucas since her glimpse of him by the shore. She *had* noticed a large study at the other end of the villa, near his bedroom suite, though. She hadn't dared to venture into his rooms, even though she'd had the opportunity when he was down by the water. Hadn't she suffered enough embarrassment for one day, with him insisting their kiss would not be repeated?

Ruby set up the dining room that was situated in the middle of the villa, overlooking the pool. The water was lit from the sides of the pool, cast in a stunning blue light. The sun was just about to sink below the horizon, painting the lower part of the sky in tangerine and pink streaks. But above that vivid colour storm clouds were forming in bruised-looking clumps, and in the distance Ruby heard a faint rumble of thunder.

Lucas came in just as she was lighting a candle in the middle of the table. He had showered and changed since she'd last seen him—his hair was still damp and curling around the collar of his light blue shirt. He was wearing dark-coloured chinos and suede loafers without socks, revealing his tanned feet. She could pick up the citrus fragrance of his cologne, the notes as intoxicating as his presence.

'Dinner won't be long. Would you like a drink?'

Who said she couldn't act cool, calm and collected after that blistering kiss?

If he was thinking about their kiss, there was no sign of it on his face.

Lucas placed his hand on the back of a chair at the dining table. 'I'll get it. What would you like? Champagne?'

'That would be lovely.'

Ruby decided against insisting she help him. The kitchen was easy to navigate, and it would be good for him to gain more independence. She stayed in the background, putting the finishing touches to their meal, but acutely aware of his every movement as he took the champagne from the wine fridge and released its cork.

But then he frowned, and turned first in one direction and then another, lines of frustration rippling across his features. 'You might have to help me find the glasses. I'm not sure where Iona has put them.'

Ruby moved over to the cupboard where she had seen the glasses earlier. 'Here we go.' She set them in front of him, standing close enough to him to see a tiny nick in the skin of his lean jaw. 'You cut yourself shaving.'

'Yes.' His mouth was pulled tight, his frown brooding.

'I could have helped you with that.'

He turned his head so he was directly facing her, his expression sardonic. 'And you could've also scrubbed my back in the shower, but I don't think that would have been a good idea, do you?'

The mocking edge to his tone did nothing to slow her pulse. And, while she knew he could only see the outline of her face, surely he could feel the searing heat coming off her cheeks? Her brain exploded with images of him naked in the shower. Images of her touching him intimately with her lips and her tongue, the steam coming off the water nothing to the sensual heat coming off their bodies.

A tiny inner demon in Ruby decided to fight back...to make him admit he was as attracted to her as she was to him. 'Because of our kiss? The kiss you say you won't let happen again even though I know you want it to?'

His hands gripped the edge of the counter, his knuckles showing white. 'You should know better than to get involved with me. I'm not your knight in shining armour.'

'Maybe not—but that's not to say we can't have a little...flirtation.'

He curled his top lip, and his pupils turned as dark and wide as black holes in space. 'A "flirtation"?'

The pitch of his voice lowered to a rough

burr that sent a shiver across the floor of her belly.

'Believe me, Ruby, you don't know what you're getting yourself in to. You'd be wise to step back right now.'

'What if I don't want to step back?' Ruby stroked her fingers down the front of his muscular chest with just enough pressure for him to feel the scrape of her nails through the light cotton of his shirt. 'What if I want to get closer? What if I want what you want?'

He sucked in a breath but didn't move away. 'I only have flings. I don't do relationships. Ever.'

Ruby sent her fingers on another exploration, this time along the strongly corded muscles of his right arm. His casual shirt was rolled back at the cuffs, revealing hair-roughened forearms. His breathing rate increased, his nostrils flaring like those of a wild stallion scenting his mate.

'So we could have a fling. While we're here on the island.'

She was a little shocked at her forthrightness. Shocked and yet secretly delighted at her brazenness. Why *shouldn't* she be honest and up-front about what she wanted? She might be an old-fashioned girl at heart, but that didn't mean she couldn't have a little fun before her handsome prince showed up, one day in the hopefully not too distant future.

She tiptoed her fingers over the back of his hand, where it was still gripping the counter, and lowered her voice to a throaty whisper. 'What happens on the island, stays on the island.'

The silence stretched and stretched and stretched, like a thin cord pulled almost to snapping point.

Then Lucas removed his hands from where they were gripping the counter and grasped her by the upper arms. His touch was electric, sending arrows of liquid heat straight to her core. He released a rush of air, as if something tightly bound inside him had suddenly given way.

'Don't say I didn't warn you when the week comes to an end.'

Then his mouth came crashing down on hers in an explosive kiss, his lips setting fire to hers. The kiss deepened with a silken thrust of his tongue through the seam of her lips. She gave a breathless gasp and surrendered to his passion—a passion that more than rivalled her own.

He slid one of his hands along the side

of her face, his touch sending shivers skittering across her scalp. He angled his head to reposition his mouth, his lips softening against hers, bewitching her into a trance-like state as hot delight shot through her body from her mouth to her curling toes and back again. An ache built in her feminine flesh…a clawing, desperate, primal need that sent pounding blood to her secretly moistening centre.

Lucas dragged his mouth off hers, his chest rising and falling against her. 'Are you sure about this? Once we do this, we can't undo it.'

His voice was rough and thick with desire, and it made her want him all the more. Ruby linked her arms around his neck, pushing her body even closer to the potent hard heat of his.

'I'm not a silly little starstruck teenager any more, Lucas. I'm a fully grown woman and I want you to make love to me—not because I'm in love with you, but because we're both attracted to each other and it makes sense to make the most of it while we can. No one will ever know.'

Lucas ran his hands down the sides of her body, his hands settling on her hips. 'As long as we're clear on the rules.'

'Do I need to sign something? A contract or a non-disclosure agreement?' Her tone was lightly teasing. 'Loosen up! I'm not going to beg you to marry me. This is just a bit of fun to pass the time.'

Lucas tugged her against him in a ruthlessly possessive fashion that sent another scalding wave of heat through her body.

'Then if it's fun you're after...'

His mouth came back down on hers in a spine-tingling kiss that sent fireworks shooting through her blood. The ache between her thighs grew to a throbbing fever-pitch, and her heart was racing as his lips and tongue wreaked sensual havoc on her senses. He growled something indistinct against her lips, a primitive sound, deep in his throat, that made the blood sing in her veins.

His mouth moved from hers to explore the sensitive skin of her neck. She rolled her head to one side, delighting in the sensual glide of his lips against her skin. He moved his mouth to just below her earlobe, his teasing touch firing up the nerves of her erogenous zones like a naked flame thrown at dry tinder.

'You smell divine...'

His voice was low and deep and thick

with desire. His teeth gently closed on her earlobe and a shiver shot down her spine like greased lightning.

'I want you so bad...' His bald statement came out like a groan of desperation.

'I want you too—just in case you hadn't noticed.'

He gave a slow smile against her lips. 'It hadn't escaped my attention.'

He kissed her deeply again, in a long, drugging kiss that ramped up her need to an unbearable level. Never had she felt such intense desire. It pounded in her body like a tribal drum.

Lucas left her mouth to kiss his way down to the top of her shoulder, his hand skilfully sliding the fabric of her shoestring-strapped sundress partway down to reveal the naked upper curve of her breast. He moved his lips across the top of her shoulder, sending shockwaves of heat through her body. She hadn't even realised her shoulder was so sensitive, but under the expert ministrations of his lips and tongue her nerves twirled and twitched and tingled.

His mouth was so close to her breast...so achingly close that her skin tightened in anticipation of his touch. He brought his hand to the globe of her breast, his touch gentle and yet no less spine-tingling. His thumb rolled back and forth over her tightly budded nipple, and a riot of sensations rippled through her.

'You're perfect…so soft and natural.'

Ruby had never seen herself as model material—in fact, she had suffered from body issues since her teens. She had more than her fair share of acne scars and cellulite, which had always made making love with someone tricky in her attempts to hide her imperfections. She knew she had never truly enjoyed sex the way it was meant to be enjoyed. She always worried that she was being assessed by her partner, compared to other far more beautiful women and found lacking. She often cut such casual encounters short by pretending to orgasm just so she could cover herself up again.

But with Lucas all those insecurities melted away. He couldn't see the tiny pockmark scars on her forehead and left cheek…he couldn't see her dimpled thighs. He could only feel his way around her body. And the way he was feeling his way around her now was thrilling beyond all measure.

'I want to touch you.'

Ruby set to work on the buttons of his shirt, desperate to place her mouth on his salty skin. She uncovered his taut and tanned chest and lowered her mouth to his sternum, licking him like a cat with slow sensual licks that evoked another guttural groan from him and a whole-body shudder.

Lucas picked her up by the waist and sat her on the counter, bunching her dress up and nudging her thighs apart so he could stand between them. He put one of his hands behind her and pushed her hard up against his body. His mouth came back down on hers, harder this time, as if his self-control was hanging by a thread. It delighted her to witness his level of arousal— to know it was *she* who was exciting him.

His mouth moved down to her uncovered breast, his lips and tongue caressing her until she was arching her back in pleasure. He stroked his hands over both her breasts, then cradled them. The gentle warmth of his touch sent a frisson of delight through her entire body. Had anyone ever paid such exquisite attention to her breasts? It was like discovering all the pleasure points of her body for the first time.

'I can tell how beautiful you are just by touching you,' Lucas said in a husky tone. 'I would normally be trying to cover myself up at this point,' Ruby confessed. 'I'm hardly supermodel material.'

He frowned. 'You shouldn't be so hard on yourself. Even most supermodels don't look like supermodels without filters and full make-up.'

Ruby stroked her hand down the length of his lean jaw, then ran her fingertip over his lower lip. 'Did you want to have dinner, or…?'

He smiled a lopsided smile and brought his mouth back down to within a centimetre of hers. 'Dinner can wait. This can't.'

And his lips covered hers in a searing kiss that set her pulses racing all over again.

There was no mistaking his intention as the breathless moments ticked on. He lifted his mouth off hers at last, and worked his way down her body with hot kisses that made her skin tingle and tighten in pleasure. He helped her wriggle out of her knickers, and then he parted her thighs and brought his mouth to the damp centre of her womanhood.

A part of her was shocked at the raw intimacy of his caresses. She had never wanted anyone to pleasure her in such a way before, but with Lucas it seemed as natural as breathing. His lips and tongue parted her swollen flesh and she shivered and shuddered in reaction. She arched her spine, resting her weight on her hands, opening her body to him in a way she wouldn't have thought possible a day ago. The sensations rippled through her in increasing waves, and then she was swept into a whirlpool of explosive feeling that sent tremors through every part of her body. Earth-shattering, mind-blowing tremors, that made her gasp and pant with wild cries of pleasure.

Lucas held her as the last of the shockwaves rolled through her. 'That was just an appetiser…'

The sexy timbre of his voice almost made her come again and Ruby gave another little shiver, her body still trying to rebalance after such a heady rush of sensations. 'I can only imagine what's for the main course, let alone dessert.'

He brushed his bent knuckles down the curve of her cheek, a lazy smile tilting his mouth. 'You sound a little undone.'

Ruby leaned her forehead on his, her breathing still ragged. 'No one has ever done that to me before…you know…like that. I've always shied away from being so…so exposed.'

He eased back to study her, and even

though she knew he could only see the vague outline of her face she sensed he was reading her all the same. Her tone, her breathing, her touch—all would be clues to her emotional state.

'Every part of you is beautiful, Ruby. Beautiful and so responsive. Do you know how much it pleases a man to have his partner receive and welcome his touch with such enthusiasm?'

'I guess I've been hooking up with the wrong men. No one has ever made me feel like that. I thought I was going to pass out with pleasure.'

Lucas smiled and placed his hands on her shoulders, bringing her closer again. 'I found it quite unforgettable too.' His voice had that sexy rough edge again.

Ruby frowned in confusion. 'But you haven't finished... I mean, I had an orgasm but you didn't—'

He placed a gentle finger over her lips. 'I can wait. You've gone to a lot of trouble with dinner. We can finish this later. In bed.'

He could wait...

Somehow his words had her self-doubts popping up their heads again like meerkats. Of *course* he could wait. He wasn't as attracted to her as she was to him. She was a convenient lover—someone he would not have looked at twice if the circumstances had been different. He normally slept with stunning model-types who hadn't a dimple of fat anywhere on their person—filter or no filter.

Ruby slipped down off the counter, hastily putting her clothes back in place, her emotions see-sawing. 'Dinner won't be long. I'm just going to…to freshen up…'

Lucas suddenly caught her by the arm as she went to go past, his fingers a steel bracelet around the slender bones of her wrist. 'You're upset.' It was a statement, not a question.

Ruby pulled her wrist out of his hold. 'Of course I'm upset. I thought you were as hot for me as I was for you, but clearly I was wrong. I'm sorry you had to suffer the indignity of…of *servicing* me.' She almost gagged on the word, but carried on regardless. 'I can assure you I won't bother you again.'

He let out a long, ragged breath. 'Sweetheart, I want you as much as you want me—even more so. But—'

'Here comes the "but",' Ruby cut in before he could finish. 'Here come the reasons why any encounter between us is inadvisable. I'm the housekeeper's granddaughter...the girl who embarrassed you all those years ago by throwing herself at you. I'm from the wrong side of the tracks. No one in your elevated circles would ever accept me as your partner. I could go on and on.'

'Please don't,' he said in a curt tone.

Ruby blinked away the sudden sting of tears, feeling her throat tighten as if something was stuck halfway down. 'I'm not beautiful. I'm ordinary. And everyone knows you don't do ordinary.'

Lucas took her by the shoulders in a gentle hold. 'Do you know how hard it's been for me to keep my hands off you from the moment you walked into the library yesterday at Rothwell Park? I couldn't see you, but I could sense you in a way I have never done with anyone else.' He gave her shoulders a light squeeze, his expression softening. 'Just because I can control my desire, it doesn't mean it's any less fervent.'

Ruby sent the tip of her tongue over her dry lips, suddenly embarrassed by her outburst. But experiencing such mind-blowing intimacy with him had made her feel incredibly vulnerable—especially since he hadn't taken his own pleasure. How could she *not* think he didn't really want her?

'I'm not used to a man taking his time with me. I haven't had a lot of lovers, and most of the ones I've had have been in a tearing rush to get their rocks off. I've mostly faked an orgasm to get it over with— especially if I could tell my enjoyment wasn't going to be a priority for them.'

Lucas framed her face in his broad hands, his features cast in lines of gravitas. 'Your enjoyment is my top priority. Otherwise there would be no point in continuing our…arrangement.'

His slight hesitation over the word he eventually used to describe their relationship made her wonder if he was regretting inviting her to his island. Everything had changed between them—especially now. *She* had changed. Her body was alive and throbbing with new energy. A sensual energy that sent her blood singing through her veins.

Ruby linked her arms around his neck. 'Do *you* want to continue?'

He lowered his mouth to just above hers. 'You bet I do.'

And then he covered her mouth with his in a kiss that left her in no doubt of it.

Lucas stood beside his bed with Ruby. His hands stroked down the length of her bare arms. Her skin was as soft as the finest quality silk. His nostrils flared to take in more of her flowery scent and he raised one of her hands to his mouth, planting a kiss on each of her fingertips in turn.

He longed to see every nuance of her expression, but he had to be content with reading her with his other senses: hearing the soft gasp of her breath as he brought her closer to his aroused body, feeling the way she moved against him, signalling her growing need, smelling the sweet musk of her arousal. Then there was the thunder of her pulse when he pressed his lips to her neck. Her sounds of encouragement…the breathless sighs and whimpers of female desire that made him want her all the more.

He placed his hands on her hips, holding her against the pounding ache of his male flesh, relishing the feminine contours of her body, delighting in the fiery chemistry that flared between them.

Lucas kissed her slowly, deeply, drinking in the milk-and-honey taste of her as if it was a drug he had never known he wanted until now. He couldn't get enough of her softness, the sweet suppleness of her lips, the shy playfulness of her tongue as it tangled with his.

He kept his mouth on hers as he helped her out of her dress, the fabric falling from her like a sloughed skin. His hands caressed the small but perfect globes of her breasts, and he lowered his head to take each tight nipple into his mouth, subjecting it to warm, moist caresses that made her whimper in pleasure.

'I love it when you do that...' she sighed.

'I love the taste of your skin,' Lucas said, trailing his lips over the upper curve of her breast. She shivered under his touch, and his body hardened even further.

'I want to taste yours.'

Ruby tugged his shirt out of his chinos and then set to work on undoing the buttons. He shrugged it off himself, impatient to have her soft little hands on his naked skin. She smoothed her hands over his pectoral muscles then, stepping on tiptoe, placed her mouth to his neck in a softly nibbling little bite that sent an arrow of lust to his groin.

'You're killing me...' He sucked in much-needed air, his body so hot, so tight, so full of thundering blood that it was part pain, part pleasure.

'That's good to know.' There was a smile in her voice...a sultry smile that made her impossible to resist even if he had wanted to.

But he didn't want to.

He had been fighting his attraction to her because he hadn't wanted any more complications in his life. But this week together on his island would be a perfect solution to scratch the itch, so to speak, and move on. End of story. No follow-ups. No promises. No relationship. No commitment.

'You're still wearing your chinos. I want to see you. *All* of you.'

Ruby wound her arms around his body, leaning into him, her nakedness thrilling him to the core. Her breasts were soft and warm against his chest, her lower body flush against his. She planted a kiss to his lips, a barely touching, teasing kiss that only ramped up his desire for more.

'That's easily fixed.'

Lucas pulled away just long enough to step out of the rest of his clothes, including his loafers. He could sense her eyes moving over every inch of him, and he waited with bated breath for her to touch him. The anticipation was intense. His body was poised, thick with blood, with pounding need, and his heart was hammering like a piston, his breathing increasingly ragged. Had he ever been this turned on before? Had anyone got him so worked up? Was it because of who she was? Someone he had known for a long time? Someone he had seen grow from child to woman?

Someone he could no longer ignore.

He couldn't see her clearly, but he could feel every sweet curve of her body. He could feel the silky texture of her skin and how it sent searing heat through his own. How could he have thought he'd be able to resist her touch? How could he have thought he had a hope of keeping his physical distance when his body craved her like a drug?

But he could still keep his emotional distance—just as he always did in his flings. He assured himself that this fling with Ruby would be no different, even though a tiny corner of his mind beeped a tiny warning sound...

He ignored it.

Ruby placed her hand on the middle of his chest, then slowly, achingly, torturously

slowly, sent it down lower, lower, lower…
until it was just above his groin.

'You're so…big…' There was a note of
awe in her voice.

'I'll take things slowly if you're nervous.'

'I'm not nervous,' she said, wrapping her
hand around his tight length. 'I'm excited.'

Lucas shuddered at her electrifying
touch. Her soft hand moved up and down,
her finger rolling over the head of his erection where pre-ejaculatory fluid oozed.

'Condom.' His voice came out hoarse, as
if his tonsils had been filed with a black-
smith's rasp. 'I need a condom.'

'Where are they?'

'In my wallet.'

Where the hell had he put his wallet?
His mind was suddenly blank. He was so
aroused there wasn't enough blood going
to his brain to get it to function.

'I've found it.' Ruby moved to the bedside table and he heard her take a condom
from his wallet, and then the soft thud as
she dropped the wallet back on the table.
'Here we go.'

She came back to him and pressed the
tiny packet into his hand.

'Why don't you put it on me?'

'Okay…'

He could imagine her biting down on her lower lip in concentration. He listened as she opened the packet, and then shivered in delight as she rolled the condom over him.

Lucas pulled her close and clamped his lips down on hers, gliding his tongue through her lips to tango with hers in a sexy duel that sent his senses into overdrive. His cupped her neat bottom with his hands, guiding her womanhood against his erection, wanting her so fiercely it was like a fever in his blood.

He finally lifted his mouth off hers, his breathing heavy. He took her hand and pulled her down to the bed. Once she was lying there he came down beside her, balancing his weight on one elbow, his other hand caressing her left breast.

'This is the first time I've made love with someone since my surgery.' Lucas wasn't sure why he was revealing such information to her, but it had come out in a moment of unguardedness.

That tiny *beep-beep-beep* in the dark corner of his mind sounded again. *Get physically close, not emotionally close.* But it was hard to keep his emotional distance with Ruby. She got under his guard like smoke under a locked door.

'Are you nervous?' The twin chord of concern and surprise in her soft voice made something in his chest contract.

'Not really. I've been making love long enough to be able to do it with my eyes closed. But it's different somehow.'

'Different in what way?'

Lucas moved his hand from her breast to the slim flank of her thigh, his expression rueful. 'It's a new experience to rely only on touch and hearing and taste and smell. I can only imagine how you look.'

'I'm kind of glad you can't see me. You might be disappointed. In fact, I'm sure you would be.'

Lucas frowned and cupped her chin in his hand. 'Stop being so negative about yourself. You are an accomplished and beautiful young woman. I've always thought so.'

'I have cellulite.'

'So? Don't most women?'

'And I have acne scars.'

'I've never noticed them.'

It was true. He hadn't. But he *had* noticed and was increasingly noticing more her emotional scars.

'Only because you've done your best to ignore me since the night of that wretched party.'

'Sweetheart, listen to me.' Lucas used

his no-nonsense tone. 'If I ignored you or avoided you it was only so you could get over your embarrassment. I didn't want to make you feel any more uncomfortable than I already had by dressing you down the way I did. Besides, I hated being at Rockwell Park—especially when my parents were there together in one of their honeymoon phases. I was always looking for excuses not to be there.'

Ruby let out a serrated sigh. 'So it's not my fault you're selling it?'

He frowned. 'How could you think it's your fault?'

He heard the movement of her shoulder against the sheet as if she had shrugged. 'I just wondered…'

He stroked his hand down her cheek. 'Stop wondering. It's strictly a business decision. I want to offload it so I can concentrate on other things. It's a white elephant to me. I'll be glad to drive out through those gates for the last time.' He leaned down to kiss her lightly on the lips. 'And speaking of concentrating on other things…' He circled the erect bud of her left nipple with his finger. 'I'm going to make love to you like you've never been made love to before.'

She gave a little shudder and nestled closer. 'That sounds exciting.'

'It will be.'

Lucas brought his mouth back down to hers, losing himself in the sweet taste of her. Her lips were soft and yet insistent, opening to him with whimper of delight that made goosebumps prickle over his skin. He positioned himself at her entrance, stroking her first with his fingers. She gasped and moved against him, urging him on with breathless sounds that jeopardised his plan to take things slowly. Her moist, fragrant heat was irresistible, and he drove forward with a deep, guttural groan of pleasure.

Her body wrapped around him, enclosing him in the tight cave of her womanhood. Shivers coursed over his flesh and his heart raced, his senses reeled and his mind whirled as he thrust and thrust and thrust in the most primal and pleasurable of dances. Ruby picked up his rhythm, moving her body with his as if they had made love together in a past life. He could hear her every breath, every gasp and whimper and cry of pleasure. He could feel the way she responded to him, and it heightened his enjoyment in a way he had not been expecting.

Lucas read the signals of Ruby's body and stroked her intimately to help her go over the edge. He held her shuddering body in his arms as her orgasm rippled through her. Her pleasure triggered his own release, and he thrust himself into oblivion with a hoarse cry. The aftershocks went on and on, until he finally collapsed, spent, satiated, stunned.

He'd been having sex for years, and yet this time it had felt...different. So different it was as if he had slipped into a parallel universe where all the rules had changed. Sex was not just about physical pleasure, but was a complex, layered experience in which body and mind were inextricably involved.

Ruby's hands moved in sensual strokes over the still-twitching muscles of his back and shoulders. 'It must've been good for you. You've got goosebumps.'

Lucas propped himself up on one elbow and used his other hand to finger-comb her silky hair. The apple scent of her shampoo teased his nostrils. 'It *was* good. Better than good.' He smiled and leaned down to kiss her soft lips.

She sighed and wound her arms around his neck, her legs still sexily entwined with his. He realised with a jolt that he didn't want to be the first to move away. He was *always* the first to move away. Always. So why wasn't he moving? Why was he holding her as if he never wanted to let her go? He would have to let her go once this week was up. That was the deal.

'It was good for me too. The best ever, in fact.'

She nestled against him and he held her close, listening to the soft and rhythmic sound of her breathing.

Lucas wasn't old-fashioned enough to be concerned about how many lovers she'd had before him. Although it was concerning that she hadn't always enjoyed sex the way it was meant to be enjoyed.

But then, wasn't that true for him too?

CHAPTER SEVEN

DINNER HAD BEEN served a little later than
Ruby had planned, but she was hardly going
to complain. She sat with Lucas in the dining room an hour or so later, her body still
tingling from his lovemaking.

Every time she thought of him possess-
ing her, a tiny frisson of pleasure coursed
through her most intimate feminine muscles. She glanced at his hand, where it was
holding his wine glass, and recalled with
another delicate shiver how it had felt to
have those clever fingers caress her.

Lucas brought his glass up to his lips and
took a sip of wine. He lowered it back to
the table, his expression somewhat preoc-
cupied. Was he already regretting the new
dynamic of their relationship?

Ruby picked up her own glass. 'You look
like you're worrying about something.'

He blinked, as if he had completely forgotten she was sitting opposite him. 'Sorry.' He gave an on-off smile. 'That was a lovely meal… thank you for going to so much trouble.'

'It was my pleasure.' She took a tiny sip of wine and then returned her glass to the table. '*Are* you worrying about something?'

He shrugged one broad shoulder. 'The usual things—work, staff issues, the sale of Rothwell Park.'

'Delphine Rainbird's wedding?'

Lucas let out a gust of a sigh. 'Not particularly. We've made a deal and I'll honour it. But don't expect me to make an appearance while it's going on. I've been to enough weddings to last me a lifetime.'

He picked up his glass again and drained the contents, setting it back down on the table with a thud that sounded as definitive as a punctuation mark.

'I love everything about weddings,' Ruby said, refusing to be put off by his brooding frown. 'Being present when two people make a permanent commitment to each other is wonderful to witness. So emotional and romantic. Of course I'm usually too busy with the catering to see as much as Harper and Aerin do, but if I haven't been able to snatch a few moments here and there I love to watch the video later.'

'Close to half of all marriages end in divorce. Those are risky odds, if you ask me.'

'I know, but most people start out with the right intentions. Few couples stand at the altar thinking they're going to get a divorce. Love doesn't always die. It gets damaged. And then pride makes people give up, instead of nurturing their relationship back to health.'

His mouth curled in a cynical manner. 'You really are a die-hard romantic.'

'I want what most people want. I want what my mother never found—nor even my gran, for that matter. I want a love that lasts, a love that heals rather than hurts, a love that builds up rather than knocks down. A love that is respectful and kind and enduring.'

'Good luck.'

Ruby pushed back her chair and began to clear the table. 'One day you're going to meet someone who challenges everything you believe to be true about relationships. It's like tempting fate to say you don't believe in love.'

He gave a half-laugh tinged with scorn. 'Isn't it tempting fate to say you do? You'll only get your heart broken.'

'And is that what scares you the most?

That your carefully guarded heart might get dented?'

There was a silence. A long awkward silence. Like a pause in the wrong place in a piece of music.

Lucas slowly rose from the table, his expression now unreadable. 'I hope you're not making the mistake of confusing great sexual chemistry for something else.'

Ruby began stacking their used plates with a noisy clatter. 'I might not have had the level of experience that you've had, but I'm not that much of a fool.'

Or was she? It would be all too easy to 'catch feelings', as the modern term went. They were having a fling, a temporary 'arrangement', but how could she protect herself from falling in love with him? He was her total opposite—an aloof cynic who had built an impenetrable fortress around his heart. She was a foolish, open-hearted, optimistic moth, and he was the bright light she could not help being attracted to, even though it might spell disaster.

'Ruby…' Lucas let out a rough-edged sigh. 'I don't want you to get hurt. You've been hurt too much already.'

'I can take care of myself.' Ruby put the plates on a tray and then turned back to him, adding, 'I've been doing it for most of my life.'

He placed his hand on her wrist. 'I know you have.'

His tone was suddenly gentle, soothing. His hand moved up to cradle one side of her face. His body was so close to hers a wave of fresh need whipped through her like a roaring backdraught of flame. His thumb moved back and forth across her cheek in a tender caress that made something in her chest spring open.

'You're brave and strong and resilient,' he said. 'So many people would have fallen at the first hurdle, but you've fought hard and fought fair to get what you want in life. I admire you for it.'

Ruby inched closer to the warmth of his body and his arms came around her and held her close. She rested her head on his chest, listening to the thud of his heart. His hand stroked the back of her head in slow, rhythmic strokes that sent shivers across her scalp and down her spine.

'The only thing that kept me going during my childhood was hope. I clung to it so desperately... I needed it like a lifeline. Each day I would wake up and pray that today would be different—that my mother would turn a corner and be the kind of mother I wanted and needed. I didn't get that wish granted, but my gran did her best to make up for it.' She glanced up at him. 'I guess hope is my default setting while cynicism is yours.'

Lucas pressed a kiss to the middle of forehead, his expression wistful. 'I wasn't always so cynical. I remember being highly optimistic as a child. But I got worn down by my parents' rocky relationship, by the broken promises they made to me and to each other. It was easier in the end not to hope at all. To wait instead for the bubble to burst—as it always did.' He let out a jagged sigh and added, 'I'm trying to be optimistic about my sight returning, but it's tough going.'

Ruby could only imagine how difficult his childhood must have been, and how those emotional wounds still impacted him today. 'Oh, Lucas…' She gently stroked his lean jaw. 'I was so envious of you, growing up at Rothwell Park. You seemed to have it all. A castle to live in, expansive grounds, money and status and two parents who loved you.'

'They didn't know how to love a child unconditionally,' Lucas said. 'They were too self-absorbed—in particular my father. My temperament was too serious for them. I think they'd imagined I would be as outgoing and gregarious as they were. They found it impossible to relate to me and I to them.'

It was a shock for Ruby to see things from his perspective. But it touched her that he felt comfortable enough to share such information with her. He had never done so before. Did that mean he was lowering his emotional guard?

'I understand now that I was only seeing the good bits,' she said. 'Not the bad bits about your life back then. Anything would have been better than what I had grown up with, and that made it harder for me to see the problems you faced for so long. And now you have to deal with the loss of your eyesight and the worry that it might not fully come back. I wish there was something I could do to help you get through this difficult time.'

He smiled a lopsided smile. 'You *are* helping. More than you probably realise.'

Ruby made a business of straightening the collar of his casual shirt. 'You don't regret bringing me here?'

He gathered her closer and rested his

chin on the top of her head. 'No. Do you regret coming?'

She leaned back to look up at him. 'You're joking, surely? What's not to love about this place? It's private, it's gorgeous, and luxurious beyond anything I've experienced before.'

There was a slight pause, and then he asked, 'Any regrets about us?'

'How can I regret having the best sex of my life?'

He cupped her left cheek in his broad hand, his expression inscrutable. 'A week is all I'm offering.'

'I know.'

Why did he have to keep reminding her? Why torture her with the clock ticking on their 'arrangement'? She knew the terms. She'd accepted the terms. Wanting more was out of the question. She knew him well enough to know he wouldn't budge on this, even though a tiny flicker of hope still burned in her chest.

His thumb moved across her cheek in an idle caress. 'Our relationship will never be the same again after this. It's not like we can go back to what we were before.' His hand fell away from her face and he stepped back. 'I need you to understand that.'

'Do you have this conversation with all your lovers?'

A ripple of tension passed over his features. 'I don't normally have a pre-existing relationship with my lovers.'

'So you only hook up with strangers? Is that what you're saying?'

'It's less complicated that way. No one gets hurt.'

Ruby resumed the task of clearing away the dinner things. 'I have nothing against casual sex, but don't you get a little tired of the…the impersonality of it?' She placed a wine glass on the tray and glanced at him. 'I mean, you never really connect with them other than physically. Doesn't that get a little boring after a while?'

He shrugged in a dismissive manner. 'Probably no more boring than having sex with the same person for years on end.'

Ruby frowned. 'But how can you say such a thing is boring when you've never been with someone long enough to get to know anything about them beyond their name? And sometimes maybe not even that?'

The line of his mouth was cynical. 'Go on believing in the fairy tale, Cinderella.

Don't let me burst your bubble. I hope you find what you want. I hope what you want actually exists.'

'It does exist for some people,' Ruby insisted. 'You mentioned the divorce rate before, but what about the percentage of couples who *do* stay together and have fulfilling and rich lives, being there for each other? I'm not talking about volatile couples, like your parents, but couples who are stable...who love each other through all of life's ups and downs. The couples whose bond is even deeper when they have children and then grandchildren. The sort of couple who love each other more each year, rather than less. Who find joy in each other...who respect each other and lovingly build their relationship as they age.'

'That's the ideal—but who's to say it's reality? Don't most people talk up their lives? Wax lyrical on social media about their so-called soul mate? What goes on behind closed doors is another story.'

Ruby let out a breath of frustration. 'I don't think I've ever met a more cynical person than you. It's like you can't allow yourself to believe in love because you know deep down it has the power to hurt you. But the thing you fear the most is often the one thing you need to embrace, in order to reach your potential.'

Lucas gave a crooked smile that didn't reach his eyes. 'You'll have your work cut out trying to convert me, Ruby. Don't waste your time and energy on a lost cause.'

He walked out without another word and Ruby's shoulders slumped on a sigh. Was she being a fool to think he had the potential to change? He had so many good qualities. He was hard-working and stable and generous, and he cared about his staff. But he stubbornly refused to believe in lasting love. His chaotic childhood would not have helped—watching his parents fall in and out of love repeatedly would have made anyone question whether love could be trusted to last. But her childhood had been even more chaotic, and way more love-deprived, and yet she was still ever hopeful of finding a soul mate.

It's not going to be Lucas Rothwell... a little voice inside her head informed her, in an unwelcome but timely dose of reality.

Their week together on his private island was not even a fling. It was an 'arrangement', so they could both achieve their goals. But how could she stop herself from wanting more? His lovemaking had shown her what had been missing in her previous relationships. He had opened up a world of sensuality to her—a dizzying world of physical delight that she knew on a cellular level she would be hard pressed to find with anyone else.

How could she want anyone else when it was Lucas who made her flesh tingle from head to toe?

How could she want any other man's lips to kiss hers when his set her on fire?

Lucas walked out to stand by the pool, listening to the rumble of thunder in the distance. A storm had been brewing for the last couple of hours, but it was still too far away for him to pick up the glare of any lightning flashes. The brooding weather seemed to match his mood, with the electrical energy in the air signalling atmospheric change a reminder of what was going on between him and Ruby.

Change that could not be reversed.

He had set a seven-day limit on their arrangement, but was a week going to be enough? The first day was almost over and he was already anticipating the next and the next and… Then what? What about when he got to day seven? Would this ache in his flesh have died down by then? Or would his body be as on fire as it was now?

He was already tempted to extend their arrangement, but he didn't want her to get the wrong impression about his motives. It had never been his intention to complicate their relationship. Hurting her was the last thing he wanted to do. She had been hurt too much already by people who should have loved and protected her. How Ruby hadn't ended up as cynical and jaded as him was a miracle, but she stubbornly refused to give up hope. Hope that one day someone would sweep her off her feet and ride off into the sunset with her.

Lucas rubbed a hand over his face and tried not to think of who that person might be. He only hoped it would be someone who took the time to understand her, to be patient and gentle with her. Someone who would admire and respect her as he did for overcoming such a rough start in life.

The sky lit up in front of him with a flash of lightning, closely followed by a booming crash of thunder. The storm was getting closer by the second.

But the savage storm in his body, and in his mind, was even closer.

Ruby turned on the dishwasher in the kitchen and just then the horizon lit up with silver swords of lightning stabbing at the sea followed by the sound of a booming crash of thunder.

She went and stood next to the open door leading to the terrace. 'Lucas? Don't you think you should come in? That storm is getting pretty close.'

He turned and came over to where she was standing, his expression difficult to read. 'Time for bed?'

She sent the tip of her tongue over her lips, feeling a wave of heat flow through her lower body. 'Did you want me to sleep in my room or...?' She left the question hanging in the air, along with her hopes.

Lucas took one of her hands and lifted it to his mouth, his lips brushing her fingers in a light caress that sent a shiver rolling down her spine.

'Or...?' There was a teasing note in his tone.

'Or...sleep in yours.'

He tugged her a little closer, bringing her

up against the deliciously hard frame of his body. 'What do you think?'

His eyes gleamed with erotic intent and her body was swamped with another tidal wave of longing. 'I think it makes sense to make the most of the time we have here.'

His gave a lazy smile. 'My thoughts exactly.'

He placed his hands on her hips, holding her against the primal throb of his body. His mouth came down and covered hers in a kiss that triggered a firestorm in her flesh. His tongue entered her mouth with the same earthy drive as his body had done, making her gasp with delight. Her tongue met his in a sexy tangle that made her blood simmer and her heart pound. Desire throbbed and pulsed between her legs with each flicker of his tongue against hers.

Another zig-zag of lightning cracked overhead, and an almost instantaneous boom of thunder. But the wild weather only seemed to heighten the electricity fizzing between their bodies.

Lucas groaned against her mouth, deepening the kiss even further, one of his hands going to the base of her spine and pressing her harder against his body. Ruby kissed him back with the same intensity, winding her arms around his neck, letting her fingers play with the curls of his hair that brushed against his collar.

He broke the kiss to bring his mouth to the neckline of her dress, his lips blazing a fiery trail across her skin. 'Ever made love in a storm before?' he asked.

'No. Have you?'

'Not that I can remember.' He nibbled on her earlobe, sending another shiver skittering down her spine. 'But first we need protection.'

Ruby glanced warily at the sky outside. 'But surely we can't get struck by lightning under the shelter of the terrace roof?'

'I meant a condom.' He nibbled her other earlobe and added, 'But making love with you *is* a little like being struck by lightning.'

'Right back at you, buddy.' Ruby gave a half-laugh. 'I don't think my body will ever be the same again.'

Lucas frowned and stroked her cheek with his index finger in a gentle touch. 'Have I rushed you? Made you sore?'

His voice was full of concern, and that made

it so much harder to control her feelings. Feelings she had promised would not exist between them during their 'arrangement'.

'No, of course not. I just meant making love with you is so different...so wonderfully different from what I've experienced before.'

What were her chances of finding such perfect chemistry with someone else? She might be an optimist, but even she could see there might be a problem finding a partner who met her needs as wonderfully as Lucas. Who else would she love as she loved him? Had she *ever* stopped loving him? Her teenage crush had simply grown into a more mature love. A love that didn't disguise his faults but accepted them as part of who he was.

But he didn't love her. He refused to love anyone. His heart was a cordoned off with razor wire.

His frown loosened, but didn't entirely disappear. He seemed to be mulling over something in that quiet, reflective manner of his. 'Promise me you won't settle for second best in your future relationships,' he said. 'Your pleasure is equally important and should never be sacrificed simply to feed a man's ego.'

'I know, but sometimes it's been hard to be totally comfortable with my partners,' Ruby said. 'I guess that can improve over time, but no one I've met so far has been worth the effort.'

His hands moved up to give her shoulders a gentle squeeze. 'Let's hope you do meet someone who's worth the effort. I hate to think of you being unhappy, Ruby.' He sighed and added, 'What's worse is the thought of me being the one to make you unhappy.'

'I understand this isn't for ever. You really don't have to keep reminding me.'

He gave an enigmatic smile. 'Perhaps it's not you I'm reminding.'

His tone had a husky edge, and he leaned down to press a lingering kiss to her mouth. Ruby's lips clung to his, her senses on high alert, her heart beating hard and heavy as his mouth moved with mastery against hers. He gave a deep sigh of pleasure and drew her closer to his body, igniting her desire like a match to kindling.

Was he rethinking the timeline on their arrangement? A week was such a short period of time. Dared she ask him to extend it? Or should she leave things as they were, hoping he would come to see the sense of enjoying the chemistry they had for a little longer?

CHAPTER EIGHT

FOUR DAYS LATER, Ruby sat by the pool watching Lucas swim lengths. By counting his strokes he was able to judge when to do a flip-turn at each end.

She would never tire of watching his lean, athletic body slicing through the water with breathtaking efficiency. His skin had developed an even deeper olive-toned tan, but due to her fairer complexion and limited swimming ability she stayed in the shade, and only jumped into the shallow end of the pool to cool off.

The week was rushing past, and he hadn't mentioned anything more about the timeline on their relationship.

Once she had meticulously gone through the builder's checklist with Lucas they had slipped into a holiday mode routine that was intensely relaxing, and a refreshing and much-needed change for her, given how hard she had been working over the last few months.

Lucas, too, looked more relaxed and at ease than he had at Rothwell Park, although there were times when she caught him staring into space with a frown on his face. She knew he was worried about his eyesight and how it would impact on his career if it didn't return. But whenever she encouraged him to talk about it he quickly changed the subject.

He was in contact with his staff via phone each day, but he kept it to a minimum and spent the rest of the time with her. They went on long walks around the island and Ruby would make a picnic to carry in a backpack, so they could lunch in the little bay on the other side of the island. She couldn't remember a time when she had felt so at ease with someone. Lucas even asked questions about her work, showing an interest in all the things she planned to do to build her business with her friends.

Lucas stopped swimming and came over to lean his forearms on the edge of the pool, close to where she was sitting. He scraped his wet hair off his face, his eyes narrowed against the bright sunlight.

'Jump in with me and cool off.'

Ruby gave a playful laugh. 'If I jump in with you I will definitely *not* be cooling off.'

His smile was broad, his teeth shining white against his tan. 'Come here.'

His tone had an arrogant note of command about it, but instead of annoying her, it excited her. A frisson of delight coursed through her and her pulse picked up its pace.

'You can't make me.'

'Can't I...?'

His silky tone sent a shockwave of lust through her core. Then he launched himself out of the pool in one supremely athletic movement, droplets of water landing on her from his glistening body.

'Hey!' She tried to shift out of the way by rolling onto one hip. 'You're making me wet.'

Lucas placed his hands on each arm of her sun lounger, effectively caging her in. 'That's the plan.' His mouth was just above hers, and his voice was deep and rough around the edges. 'I love it when you're wet for me.'

Ruby shivered, and couldn't take her eyes off his mouth. The smiling contours of his sculpted lips sent hot pulses of need through her. Those lips had been on the most intimate parts of her body, sending her to paradise and beyond so many times she had lost count.

She linked her arms around his neck, bumping her lips against his once, twice, three times. 'I want you.'

He smiled against her lips. 'I want you more.'

She reached down and stroked the thickened ridge of his erection, smiling a sultry smile. 'Mmm, what's got you all excited?'

'You.'

Lucas adjusted the sun lounger so it reclined a little further, then pushed her legs apart and kneeled between them. He stroked the seam of her body through her bikini bottoms, the light caress sending shivers cascading down her spine and tightening every nerve in her pelvis in anticipation. Then he nudged the fabric aside and placed his mouth on her most intimate flesh. He tasted her, teased her, tantalised her. Until she was sobbing with pleasure, her whole body shaking, as the rippling, rolling, crashing waves smashed through her.

Ruby finally managed to sit upright, her senses still reeling, her body experiencing delicious little aftershocks. 'I can't let you get away with rendering me senseless without some sort of payback…' She sprang off the sun lounger and commanded him, 'Lie down.'

Lucas lay in the space she had just vacated. 'Should I be nervous?'

'Very.'

He gave a whole-body shudder and sucked in a breath. 'I can hardly wait.'

Ruby worked her way down his body from his mouth to his bellybutton and back again, in teasing kisses and caresses that made his breathing rate escalate. Then, on her next journey down his body, she went a little lower, stopping just above the jut of his erection.

'You're torturing me…' he groaned, and gripped the edges of the sun lounger as if to anchor himself.

'That's the plan…' She echoed his own words and then, kneeling down beside him, licked along his skin from the shallow cave of his bellybutton to the hem of his swimming trunks. Then slowly, ever so slowly, she peeled his trunks down, her gaze drinking in the potent length of him. 'Mmm… now, where will I start?' she mused, trailing a lazy finger from the head to the base of his erection and then back again.

He gave another shudder and muttered a curse-word, his body twitching in anticipation. Ruby placed her mouth on him, licking and stroking him with the tip of her tongue, delighting in the guttural groans he was making, delighting in the thrill of pleasuring him in a way she had not done with anyone before. It had always seemed too raw and intimate, and yet with Lucas she relished the texture of his skin and the taste of his essence.

She worked on him until he was close to the edge, his groans increasing with each silky movement of her mouth against his rigid flesh. And then he finally let go, his body racked with a series of violent shudders. She watched the flickering emotions on his face—the agony, the ecstasy, the exhilaration, and then finally the relaxation.

Lucas opened his eyes and turned his head towards her. One of his hands came up and touched her lightly on the face, her nose, her lips her chin. 'That was...amazing. *You* are amazing.'

Ruby shrugged. 'Not bad for a beginner, I suppose.'

He frowned. 'You mean you haven't ever—?'

'No. You're the first partner I've wanted to do that to. It never felt right for me before.'

He finger-combed her hair back from her face, his expression thoughtful. 'It's not an experience I'm going to forget in a hurry.' He let out a shuddery breath and added, 'But then, there's a lot about this week I'm not going to forget.'

Ruby sat on the edge of the sun lounger next to him and tiptoed her fingers down his forearm. 'It's going so quickly...'

'Yes...'

A silence fell.

'Ruby?'

'Yes?'

He stroked his hand up and down the length of her arm from shoulder to wrist. 'Thank you for being with me this week. It's been what I needed—some time out to think about my situation going forward.' He gave a rueful smile and added, 'If it hadn't been for you coming that day to Rothwell Park and asking about Delphine's wedding, I would probably still be sitting brooding on my own in the library.'

'Why did you ask me to come with you?'

He moved his head in a side-to-side motion, as if trying to think of an appropriate answer. 'The builder's checklist had to be done… But truly I didn't intend for anything like this to happen between us.' He ran a lazy finger over the slope of her left breast. 'Or at least that's what I told myself. But I found it hard not to kiss you, to want you… And when you seemed to want me just as much—well, I figured it was the perfect opportunity to indulge in a fling.'

'Is that what we're calling it now? A "fling"? I thought it was an "arrangement".' Ruby kept her tone light and teasing.

His mouth twisted again. 'I'm not sure what to call it any more.' He brushed his finger over her lower lip, his expression cast in contemplative lines. 'You're not like any other lover I've had in the past.'

'Yes, well, that's because I've never gone near a catwalk in my life and nor am I ever likely to.'

Lucas took one of her hands and gave it a gentle squeeze. 'I wish you wouldn't be so negative about yourself. I've met stunning women who have bored me within seconds. You're both beautiful *and* interesting.' His other hand came up to cup her cheek. 'And so sexy I can barely keep my hands off you.'

But how beautiful would he think her if he got his sight back?

She was not in the same class of attractiveness as his usual partners by any stretch of the imagination. And her insecurities were hard-wired into her personality—drummed into her by the cruel comments of her mother and many of her unsavoury boyfriends. And if Lucas thought her so irresistible, why had he placed such a strict time limit on their relationship?

A soft little sigh escaped from Ruby's lips. 'You're great for my ego. I don't think I've ever had so many nice things said to me in my entire life.'

Lucas continued to hold her hand. 'I guess your gran isn't one to splash compliments about. But she loves you and is enormously proud of you.'

'I know…but there's a part of me that feels unlovable. I mean, if my own mother couldn't love me, who else could?'

'It's understandable you feel like that, given what you've been through.' His thumb stroked the back of her hand in a soothing fashion. 'But you can't let your mother's inadequacies as a parent dictate your life going forward. She might not have been capable of loving you, or anyone, but there are plenty of other people who are.'

But he wasn't one of them, was he? He

liked her, and he enjoyed her company, but he didn't love her the way she wanted to be loved. Was it because of the way he'd seen love growing up? The way it had been expressed via his parents?

The sound of a mobile phone ringing sounded in the ensuing silence.

'That's my phone,' Ruby said, reaching for her sarong. 'I'd better answer it. It might be Gran calling.'

She got to her phone on the table inside the villa just in time to see it was Aerin on the line.

'Hi, Aerin.'

'I have good news and bad news—which do you want first?'

'Let's go with the bad news.'

'Delphine wants to bring the wedding forward.'

Ruby frowned. 'Forward by how much?'

'She wants to get married next weekend.'

'Next weekend?' Ruby's response came out as a squeak. 'Are you serious?'

'Apparently there's been a sudden change in the shooting schedule for the movie she's filming, so the wedding has to be brought forward. It's the only time she has available now. It's going to be a nightmare to pull it off, but I think we can do it. Harper is okay with the change. And we don't have any other bookings next weekend, so there's no reason why we can't rise to the challenge.'

Ruby had every confidence that Aerin would be able to pull it off, and Harper was always one to be prepared for a sudden change in plan. But would Lucas be okay with the change? She would have to fly back tomorrow to organise her catering team. Catering for a wedding was not as easy as putting a picnic together. There was so much planning and preparation to do before the event. And she would have to make sure the cleaning team had left Rothwell Park in tiptop shape…

'So what's the good news?'

'Delphine insists on paying us a bonus for the date-change.' Aerin named a figure that made Ruby's eyebrows lift. 'I told her I'd check with you first, before I confirmed it.'

'We'd be crazy not to accept,' Ruby said. 'Tell her it's a yes.'

She ended the call and glanced at Lucas, still lying on his back on the sun lounger out on the terrace, his hands propped behind his head, his eyes closed against the bright sunlight.

She walked back out to him and he

opened his eyes and reached for one of her hands. 'How's your gran?'

'It wasn't my gran.' She sat down beside him. 'Lucas, there's been a change of plan. Delphine wants to get married this coming weekend instead of next month. I'll have to fly back tomorrow to get ready. I know we agreed on a week here together, but I have so much to do...'

Lucas sat upright and laced his fingers through her hair in a light caress that sent shivers across her scalp. If he was disappointed that their week was being cut short he didn't show it on his face.

'I'll call Stavros to pick us up first thing tomorrow. Will you be able to do everything you need to do in such a short time?'

'I think so. I've done a couple of big weddings at short notice before. And it will be easier doing it at Rothwell Park because I know the kitchen so well. But it's still a huge challenge.'

He gave a crooked smile and stroked a lazy finger down the slope of her nose. 'I'm sure you're more than up to it.'

Ruby bit her lip. 'Lucas...you know how we agreed that what happens on the island, stays on the island...? I'm sorry for cutting our time together short by three days, but—'

He captured her hand and entwined his fingers with hers. 'We don't have to cut it short.'

She blinked and swallowed. Could this mean he was keen to continue their relationship? Hope flared in her chest and she felt a bubble of excitement in her blood. 'What do you mean?'

'We can continue our arrangement.'

Her heart skipped a beat. 'Until when?'

His expression gave nothing away. 'Let's leave it open-ended for now. The sale of Rothwell Park will be finalised in the next few weeks, so I'll be moving out. And you'll have to head back to London in any case.'

Her hope lost some ground, sinking back down to reality with a painful thud.

'You'll have to head back to London in any case.'

She'd be going alone.

Lucas was only offering her an extension on their arrangement. An extension was good, but the timeline was still in place—a definitive timeline that left her wanting more. Aching for more.

She looked down at her hand, encased in his large one, and something in her chest tightened like a vice. 'And where will you go?'

'That depends.'

She glanced up at him. 'On whether you regain your sight?'

'Yes…' His tone was weighted, and a flicker of worry passed over his features.

Ruby stroked a hand down his jaw. 'You mustn't give up hope. It might not return as soon as you want, but hopefully it *will* return.'

His smile was not quite a smile. 'I'll just have to wait and see.' His mouth twisted further, and he added with unmistakable irony, 'Or not.'

Ruby was relieved to find, once they got back to Rothwell Park, that the cleaning and gardening teams had done a brilliant job. The castle sparkled from top to bottom, and there wasn't a weed or blade of glass out of place in the expansive gardens. Even the weather had brightened. There were no gloomy clouds on the horizon, no threat of rain, and while the air was still cool, the sun was out in a clear blue sky.

Her gran had left hospital and was staying with a friend in the Lake District, seemingly enjoying her new, quieter pace of life. Ruby's team were arriving the following day, as well as Aerin and Harper, which left only tonight for her to be truly alone with Lucas before all the frenetic activity began.

She was still blissfully relieved about him extending their arrangement. She had been so sure he would stick to his plan of *What happens on the island, stays on the island.* Could it mean he was developing feelings for her? More lasting feelings? It was hard not to cling to hope, for he made love to her with such exquisite attention to her needs.

Their physical chemistry was unquestionably divine, but his companionship was also something she found increasingly enjoyable. Their chats over dinner or on their long walks had opened her up to his world of landscape design, and the worries he had about resuming his career if his sight didn't return. His willingness to share such moments of vulnerability with her made her feel closer to him than she had felt to anyone else—even, to some degree, her two best friends.

Ruby was finding it impossible to imagine going back to her single life now that she had experienced being in a fulfilling relationship, even if it had only been for a few days. It was a world apart from any relationship she'd had before, so how could she not hope it would continue, perhaps for ever?

Lucas had taken himself off to the library to make some phone calls to his staff a couple of hours ago, so Ruby set a tea tray and took it in to him. The door was ajar, so she nudged it further open and carried the tray over to the windows, where he was standing with his back to the room. He turned and faced her, a smile relaxing his features.

'Tea for two?'

'Yes, because tomorrow this place will be crawling with people.' Ruby set the tray down and picked up the teapot. 'Thank you for being so good about the sudden change. And about allowing us to use Rothwell Park. It's a dream come true for us to host such a big celebrity event.'

His smile became twisted. 'As long as you don't expect me to make an appearance. Weddings bring me out in hives.' He stood next to one of the chairs and she handed him a cup of tea. 'Thanks.' He took the cup and waited for her to take a seat before he too sat.

Ruby picked up a teaspoon and stirred her own cup of tea. She put the spoon down again and took a sip, watching him over the rim of her cup. A frown was carved on his forehead and one of his fingers was tapping the side of his cup in a restless manner.

She put her cup on the table between them. 'Is everything okay?'

He blinked and reset his features into a less brooding expression, but she could still see shadows moving behind his gaze. 'Just work stuff. A project that needs my attention. But what can I do?' He let out a sigh of frustration. 'Clearly nothing at the moment.'

'Oh, Lucas, it must be so frustrating for you. I wish there was something I could do to help.'

'You've already helped more than I can say.' He let out a long sigh and leaned forward to place his own cup on the table. He sat back and continued in a wry tone, 'Patience was never one of my strong points.'

Ruby stood and went over to stand by his chair, stroking his ink-black hair, her body pressed close to his side. One of his arms came around her waist and a thrill went through her at his touch.

He pulled her down to his lap, one of his hands cradling the side of her face. 'You're very good at distracting me.'

'Am I?'

He pressed a soft kiss to her lips. 'You know you are.'

'I find you pretty distracting too.'

'All the more reason for me to stay out of the way while you do your wedding preparations.'

Ruby stroked the hair back from his forehead. 'I'd like you to meet Aerin and to say hi to Harper again.'

His brows snapped together. 'Why?'

'Because we're using your family home as a wedding venue and they'd like to thank you for your generosity.'

He dislodged her from his lap and stood and went to stand at the windows again, his back turned towards her. 'You can thank me for them.'

'But it would be so nice for them to—'

He swung back to face her, his expression set in intransigent lines. 'What have you told them about us?'

'Nothing.'

He gave a rough-sounding laugh. 'How did you explain our days on the island?'

Ruby licked her suddenly dry lips. 'I didn't tell them about your eyesight, and I didn't tell them we were having a fling. In fact, they both warned me against doing any such thing.'

'Maybe you should've heeded their warning.'

'Maybe I should have.'

She stood and began clearing away the tea things, feeling her heart contract at the way he was pushing her away. But how could she regret some of the most magical days of her life? Days filled with sensual pleasure and delight. Days she would remember for ever.

Lucas let out a stiff curse-word and came over to her. He placed his hands on the tops of her shoulders and turned her to face him. 'I'm sorry for being in such a foul mood.' He gave her shoulders a gentle squeeze and added, 'Thank you for keeping my condition a secret from your friends. I can't bear people's pity.'

Ruby wound her arms around his waist and laid her head on his chest. 'I understand. I'd probably be the same.'

He held her close for endless seconds, then he eased back to lift her face with a finger beneath her chin. He searched her features, as if willing his eyes to see her more clearly. But maybe it was better that he couldn't, for she was finding it hard to hide the feelings she had for him. The feelings that had grown against her will, against her better judgement, against the advice of her best friends, against all reason. Feelings that could not be so easily dismissed as a silly little teenage crush. Feelings that were deep and strong and yet painful, because she was gambling on the slim chance that he might one day return them.

His lashes lowered to half-mast over his eyes and his mouth came down on hers in a kiss that melted her bones and curled her toes and sent her pulse racing off the charts. His tongue glided into her mouth to mate with hers in an erotic dance that sent blazing heat to her core. His arms moved around her, bringing her closer to the hard frame of his body. He groaned against her mouth—a guttural groan that spoke of urgent primal need spiralling out of control. The same primal need that was barrelling through her body in tidal waves of searing, blistering heat.

'I can't stop wanting you,' he said, in a tone that seemed to hint at deep frustration with himself.

'I want you too,' Ruby said. 'So much it hurts.'

He held her face between his hands, angling her head so he could deepen their kiss. The kiss went on and on, sending her senses into a tailspin. His lips were soft and cajoling, and then hard and insistent, ramping up her need for him to fever-pitch. He lowered his mouth to the sensitive skin of her neck, the teasing movement of his lips sending shivers down her back. He set to work on her clothes and she worked on his, her hands less efficient than she would have liked. But finally they were both naked and Lucas had sourced a condom.

'You came prepared,' Ruby said with a sultry smile.

'I've learned to be prepared around you. You turn me on in a heartbeat.'

Lucas lowered his mouth to the curve of her right breast, his tongue circling her nipple in a spine-tingling caress. He took the nipple gently between his teeth, then sucked on her, drawing her nipple further into the warm cave of his mouth. Hot arrows of pleasure shot through her body and molten heat pooled in her core. He moved to her other breast, subjecting it to the same deliciously erotic caress, and she felt her legs weakening as the pleasurable sensations rippled through her in waves.

Lucas guided her down to the floor and then came down beside her in a tangle of limbs. He stroked her hair back from her face, his eyes glazed with lust. 'Are you sure you don't want to take this upstairs, to a comfortable bed?'

'No time for that.' She pulled his head down so his mouth came back to hers.

His kiss was long and deep, his breathing as hectic as hers. Then he thrust into the seam of her body with a harsh groan. 'You feel so damn *good*...'

Ruby caught his fast rhythm, her body gripping him, wanting him, needing him. His thrusts became deeper, harder, faster, but she was with him all the way. Her senses were on fire as the pressure built in her most intimate flesh. She was wet and swollen, tight with need. He placed a hand beneath one of her buttocks to lift her pelvis to receive him deeper, and the friction intensified, electrifying. Tiny flickers of pleasure became a ferocious fireball of flames and flashing fireworks as her orgasm swept through her. She gasped out loud as the sensations exploded in her flesh, her body thrashing beneath his as the waves pulsed through her. Lights flashed behind her closed eyes and scorching heat flowed to every inch of her body.

Lucas followed with his own explosive

release, his harsh cries echoing in the cavernous silence of the library. He collapsed on top of her, his head against the side of her neck, his warm breath a caress on her skin. 'Am I too heavy for you?'

'No.'

'Good, because I don't think I can move right now.'

Ruby stroked her hands over the taut muscles of his back and broad shoulders, a smile curving her mouth. 'Nice to know I have that effect on you, since you do the same to me.'

There was a peaceful silence.

Lucas finally propped himself up on one elbow, his free hand lazily stroking the curve of her cheek, his expression suddenly serious. 'I wish I could see you more clearly.'

There was a note of wistfulness in his tone that plucked at her heartstrings.

'I can tell when you're smiling, but that's about all.'

Ruby brushed his lower lip with her index finger. 'I have more freckles since we got back from Greece.'

'Where?'

'On my nose.'

He bent down and kissed the bridge of her nose. 'I've always found your freckles kind of cute.'

He placed another kiss at the corner of her mouth, setting every nerve on high alert.

'In fact, there's not a part of you I don't find irresistibly attractive.'

And his mouth came down to cover hers again.

During the early hours of the morning, Lucas woke from a deep and restful sleep to find Ruby nestled against him, fast asleep. He ran an idle hand up and down the silky skin of her arm, breathing in the honey-suckle scent of her body, feeling her fragrant hair tickling his nostrils where her head was tucked below his chin. He never failed to marvel at the texture of her skin, the sweet taste of her lips, the sensual warmth of her body. He couldn't get over the way she responded to him with such enthusiasm and delight. His desire for her hadn't abated at all—it had become more fervent.

He began to drift back to sleep, but then a worry began to nibble at the wainscoting of his mind…

He had done something he had never done before. He had extended a fling with a lover. Not only extended it, but left it open-ended. Before now, even if he hadn't actually told a lover their end date, he had always had one sketched in his mind. But with Ruby it was as if his playboy rulebook had been torn up. He had ignored his own rules, put them to one side, in order to indulge in a fling that wasn't like any other fling he'd had before.

Was it because she wasn't a stranger he had met in a bar? She wasn't a casual lover—someone who wanted a good time not a long time? Ruby was after the damn fairy tale, and yet he was drawn to her by an irresistible force he couldn't explain, let alone control. Was it because he already had a relationship with her? One that went back years? Was that what was making it so freaking hard to define a timeline? Or was it the mind-blowing sex between them that kept getting better and better?

He couldn't remember having a partner who was so in tune with him physically. He was no stranger to good sex—great sex, even. But with Ruby it was on a whole new level. Was it because he couldn't see her but only feel her? Because he could only taste and smell and touch her? Had his other senses intensified the experience, making him wonder if making love with anyone else was going to be as good, regardless of whether he got his sight back?

Ruby murmured something and nestled closer. He felt something in his chest flare open, and a sensation of warmth seeped into all the cold corners of his guarded heart.

Careful, buddy, don't let things get too serious. Don't get too close. A fling is a fling, no matter how long or short it is. Stay in control.

Lucas dismissed the warning of his conscience. Of course he was still in control. He wasn't going to let things get out of hand just because he had extended the timeframe on his relationship with Ruby. He might be enjoying the explosive chemistry between them, but that didn't mean he was losing control of his emotions.

He *never* lost control of his emotions.

Falling in love was something that happened to other people, not him. He had a line drawn in his mind and nothing and no one was going to make him step over it. Ruby might be refreshing and endearing and super-sexy, but he wasn't going to suddenly morph into a knight in shining armour.

Not now. Not ever.

Not possible.

CHAPTER NINE

RUBY WELCOMED HER best friends and business partners to Rothwell Park the following day, along with her catering team. Once her team were busy setting up in the kitchen she met with Aerin and Harper in the less formal of the three sitting rooms, for a quick catch-up over drinks and nibbles.

'These look scrumptious,' Harper said, reaching for one of the savoury tartlets Ruby had prepared earlier. 'There goes my diet. I'm so hungry I could eat a horse and chase the rider—and maybe the saddle and bridle wouldn't be safe from me either.'

'You don't need to diet,' Aerin said with a tinkling bell laugh. 'I think you look amazing right now. Your skin is glowing and your hair is so shiny. Have you had a treatment?'

'Yes, I was thinking so too,' Ruby said. 'I don't think I've seen you look better.'

Harper took another tartlet off the plate and waggled her eyebrows at Ruby. 'I could say the same about you. Four days on a private Greek island with Lucas Rothwell seems to have agreed with you. So, when do we meet him?' She popped the tartlet in her mouth and chewed with obvious enjoyment.

'He's not feeling very sociable at the moment,' Ruby said, hoping her hot cheeks weren't giving her away. 'Weddings kind of freak him out, given how his parents married and divorced each other three times.'

How else could she explain why he wouldn't meet them? She hadn't told them he was blind, after his request for privacy.

But Harper had obviously picked up on something, for she leaned forward with a narrowed look. 'What's going on? There's something you're not telling us.'

'Nothing's going on,' Ruby said, averting her gaze.

'So how was it? The island?' Aerin asked, her eyes wide with interest.

'Amazing.' Ruby took a parmesan sablé off the platter and put it on her plate. 'The villa is gorgeous, and it has a wonderful infinity pool set in front of it, so most of the rooms on that side of the villa look out over it. The gardens aren't fully grown, but they'll be a showpiece once they're established. There are several lovely beaches, and there's a long private jetty and a pine forest that covers almost two-thirds of the island. I'll show you photos later. But first we'd better run through the wedding programme.'

The less she talked about Lucas and the island, the better. Revealing too much of her relationship with him would mean revealing her feelings about him. Her friends had already warned her about losing her heart to a man who couldn't commit.

Harper stopped raiding the platter to fix her gaze on Ruby. 'So, did you sleep with him?'

Ruby was aware of the heat storming in her cheeks. 'I don't want to talk about it. Look, we have Delphine's wedding in a day's time and—'

'You did!' Harper said, slapping her own knee. 'I knew you wouldn't be able to resist him. Don't say I didn't warn you.'

Aerin had a look of concern on her face. 'Are you *still*…sleeping with him?'

Ruby blew out a breath. 'We were only going to have a fling while we were on the island, but then we had to come back early for Delphine's wedding, and now...'

'So, that's a yes,' Harper said. 'Well, I guess it's your life and your heart and all that. But I can't see it ending well—especially if he doesn't want to be seen in public with you while you're together.'

Aerin chewed at one side of her mouth, her gaze steady on Ruby. 'You're in love with him, aren't you? I mean, *really* in love.'

Ruby let out another long sigh. 'I tried so hard not to fall for him, but I guess I've always had feelings.' She picked up her drink and stared at the contents for a moment before adding, 'Not that he returns those feelings. We're just having a fling, that's all. That's all he ever has—flings.'

'I know the type,' Harper said with an eyeroll, but then continued in a more compassionate and reflective tone. 'It really sucks to fall for someone who's unattainable. But sometimes I wonder if that's what happens to former care home kids like us. The people we loved as kids didn't love us the way we were supposed to be loved, so we tend to fall for men who are the same. Totally unattainable men who are not able to love us the way we want to be loved.'

Ruby frowned in confusion. 'Are you saying you're in love with Jack Livingstone?'

Harper rapid-blinked, like an animal sure it was about to become roadkill, and then she screwed up her face in distaste. 'No, of course not.'

'I think you're both being a little hard on Lucas and Jack,' Aerin said. 'Not all playboys stay unattached for the rest of their lives. Look at my dad, for instance. He was a notorious playboy until the day he met my mum. Then he couldn't get a ring on her finger quick enough, and they're still as in love as the day they met.' She gave a dreamy sigh and added, 'Wouldn't it be wonderful if all three of us could find a partner like that?'

'Personally, I'm happy on my own,' Harper said. 'Call me hypocritical for working as a wedding photographer, but I don't want the complications of fitting my life around some guy who expects his pipe and slippers brought to him each night.'

'I think most men are a little more woke than that these days,' Aerin said with a light laugh. 'But seriously, Ruby...' Her expression sobered. 'Only you can decide what to do. But it seems to me a positive thing Lucas wants to continue the fling.'

'I know… But, like Harper said, I've had a lifetime of getting my hopes up only to have them dashed,' Ruby said. 'Lucas has always been a closed-off sort of person, but he's opened up about a bit of stuff over the last few days—about his childhood and his parents and their crazy relationship. And, to be honest, I too have shared things I've only ever shared with you two before. I kind of feel Lucas and I have got to know each other on a different level. A more intimate level.'

'Yes, well…if you're getting naked with him, it doesn't get more intimate than that,' Harper put in.

'I think it's more than that,' Ruby said. 'I feel more comfortable around him than ever before. And I think he does around me.'

'Do you feel comfortable enough to tell him how you feel about him?' Aerin asked.

'I don't know…' Ruby chewed at her lower lip, wondering how Lucas would take it if she told him how she felt. Would he reject her as brutally as he had all those years ago? He had told her the rules—and yet he had changed the rules…a little. Only a little, but that fed her hopes. Or was she being foolish to hope his locked-away heart could ever be opened?

Opened to *her*?

Lucas was in his study when Ruby came in, just before dinner. She closed the door behind her with a soft little click. She approached his desk and, although he could only see the blurry outline of her body, he could see she was wearing a baby blue dress. He would enjoy taking her out of it later. He caught a whiff of her peony and tuberose perfume and his senses reeled.

'Have your friends settled in?' he asked.

'Yes. I put Aerin in the blue room and Harper in the yellow room.' She paused for a beat and added, 'I told them you weren't feeling very sociable at the moment and don't like weddings. I couldn't think of any other excuse for why you weren't keen to meet them.'

A twinge of guilt jabbed him for being so hardnosed about keeping out of everyone's sight. 'I'm sorry, but it's best if I stay in the background.'

He heard the floorboards creak as she shifted her weight from foot to foot. He sensed she had something to confess. He could read the little tell-tale signs so well—the hitched in-breath, the rustle of her clothes, the wringing of her hands.

'Lucas...? I'm sorry, but I did tell the girls about us...about our fling. But they won't tell anyone else. I trust them to keep it out of the media.'

Lucas let out a stiff curse-word and rolled his chair back from the desk. 'Was it necessary to tell them? They're only here for a couple of days. Surely you could have kept it a—'

'I don't know how close you are to *your* friends, but, no, I couldn't keep it from them,' Ruby said in a tight little voice. 'In any case, they guessed—or at least Aerin did.'

'Guessed?'

He was so attuned to her he heard her lips part softly before she spoke. 'I didn't realise having amazing sex for the first time in my life would leave signs upon my person, but apparently it has.' Her tone was decidedly wry.

Lucas moved to where she was standing. He slowly stroked his hands down the length of her arms and then captured her wrists. 'I'm sorry for being touchy about my privacy. I just want to keep my private life out of the press—but not because I don't want to be seen with you.'

'I understand...'

Lucas put his finger beneath her chin and lifted her gaze to his blurry one, wishing with all his heart he could see her expression in finer detail. 'Do you?'

Her tongue slipped out and swept across her lips. 'I'm not sure it's going to do my image much good being seen with you, either.'

He frowned. 'What do you mean?'

'I'm in the wedding business. What does it say about me that I'm having a fling with a playboy who's made it perfectly clear he will never settle down?'

Lucas tightened his hold on her wrists as the blood thickened in his veins. Being this close to her always sent his blood racing south. He was addicted to her and he could do nothing to stop it. It was a fever in his system—a raging fever that took over his rational brain, pushing aside all his reasons for keeping his distance.

He didn't *do* long flings, and yet he was already thinking of ways to keep her with him. Not for ever, but for longer than he would normally consider. He was starting to find it hard to imagine making love with anyone else. That had never happened to him before. In the past, the lure of the next lover had always pulled him forward.

But not this time—which was deeply concerning. He had to get a grip and keep control of this escalating need for her before it got out of hand. A fling was a fling, no matter if it lasted a week, a month or a couple of months.

He was *not* falling in love.

'I hardly think people are going to judge you for having a bit of fun,' he said.

Ruby moved a little closer, and he felt her lower body igniting his with flickering flames of lust.

'Is that all I am to you? A little bit of fun?' Her tone was light and playful, but he sensed a chord of disquiet underneath.

Lucas released her wrists and framed her face in his hands. 'You are way much more than that.'

And then his mouth came down on hers like a magnet drawn to metal. Her lips tasted of strawberries, and he wondered if he would ever eat that fruit again without thinking of her. His tongue met hers in an erotic dance that made a tingle move down his spine and the backs of his legs.

No, he was not falling in love. But he was falling deeper in lust.

And, if he was any judge, so was she.

The day of Delphine Rainbird's wedding arrived and Ruby was up before dawn, working with her team in the kitchen. The florist had been the day before and the castle looked stunning, with whimsical floral arrangements everywhere. The ballroom where the reception was being held looked like a fairyland, with gleaming candelabra on the tables and scattered rose petals in an array of colours. The silverware was polished and the starched white tablecloths were set with silver-embossed crockery.

Ruby wished Lucas could see everything, but even if he had his sight she knew he would avoid coming anywhere near the wedding. It would be too triggering for him, given the three weddings of his parents, all held at Rothwell Park, and all subsequently ending in acrimony and bitterness.

Harper came in with her camera bag and a sophisticated digital camera slung around her neck. 'Looks fabulous, Ruby. I'm heading upstairs to take some shots of Delphine and her bridesmaids getting ready. It's great that the weather's looking good.'

Ruby glanced out of the windows and smiled. 'Yes, but Delphine's so happy she wouldn't mind if it was sleeting or snowing outside.'

'Miguel seems pretty chuffed too,' Harper said, fiddling with the settings on her camera.

'Yes…' Ruby bent down to pick up a stray rose petal from the floor and held it to her nose, sniffing the clove and peppery smell of an old English rose.

'Are you okay?'

Ruby put the petal on the table nearest her and turned to look at her friend. 'I'm fine. Tired, though. I barely slept last night.'

Harper raised her eyebrows. 'Let me guess—not because you're nervous about the wedding, but because you were in Lucas Rothwell's bed, having amazing sex till the wee hours?'

Ruby's cheeks were so warm they threatened to wilt the rose petals. 'I know you don't approve, but I can't seem to help myself.'

Harper let out a heartfelt sigh. 'I do know what that feels like. That night I slept with Jack…' Her brow furrowed into a frown of self-disapproval. 'It was like I had zero self-control. I still can't believe I had a one-night stand with him—with anyone, for that matter. And at a wedding, for God's sake. A wedding where I was supposed to be working—not cavorting with the best man.' She blew out a breath and side-eyed Ruby. 'I left one of my favourite earrings in his hotel room.'

'Have you got it back?'

'No.'

'Why not?'

Harper's expression tightened. 'Because he insists on giving it back to me in person, and I don't want to see him again.'

'Do you want me to get it for you?'

Harper aimed her camera at the bridal table and took a couple of shots. 'I've already suggested that, but he was pig-headed about it and said I could only get it back if I agreed to see him. So—goodbye, favourite earring.'

Ruby had known Harper long enough to know how stubborn she could be when she made up her mind about something. 'You're not only being hard on Jack, you're being hard on yourself,' she told her. 'You're only human, and he *is* pretty darn hot.'

Harper made a scoffing noise and took another round of photos. 'I've taught myself to resist hot men.'

'Good luck with that,' Ruby said in a wry tone. 'That's not quite working for me at the moment.'

Lucas could hear the wedding in full swing downstairs but he stayed in his study, trying not to remember the wild celebrations of his parents as they'd repeated their mistakes time and time again. If that was love, then he wanted nothing to do with it.

There was a tap at the door and he stiffened in his chair. He had told Ruby no one was to be allowed in this part of the castle. Was a member of the press snooping about in his private quarters? It reminded him of being chased by the media as a child, cornered like a terrified animal, cameras pointed at him like guns.

Would he be tomorrow's biggest headline? Would his health issue be splashed over every media outlet? Why had he agreed to this damn wedding being hosted here? He should have known it would come to this. That some sneaky journalist would hunt him down and—

'Lucas? It's me,' Ruby said. 'I've brought you something to eat and drink.'

He breathed out a sigh of relief and rose from his chair to go and unlock the door.

But his emotions were still in disarray. Emotions he didn't want to acknowledge. Vulnerability being at the top of the list.

Ruby was carrying a loaded tray of delicious-smelling food and he suddenly realised he was starving. Not just for food but for her company. It had been hours since she'd left his bed that morning. Long, boring hours of him aching for her. Wanting her. Needing her and being angry with himself for it. Furious that he was finding it so hard to resist her. Annoyed with himself for being more in lust with her than ever.

He moved out of her way so she could put the tray on his desk. 'You shouldn't have bothered. Aren't you supposed to be working?' His tone was brusque and unwelcoming, but he couldn't get his heartrate back to normal.

Ruby put the tray down and turned to look at him. 'My team have got everything under control.'

Unlike him. He was so out of control emotionally he could barely think straight.

'Are you okay?'

Lucas scraped an impatient hand through his hair. 'Of course I'm okay. There's a freaking celebrity wedding downstairs that sounds exactly like my parents' ones.

Why *wouldn't* I be okay? I just hope they've drawn up an ironclad prenuptial agreement, because we both know how this is going to end.'

'They have,' Ruby said matter-of-factly. 'Have you heard of Drake Cawthorn, the celebrity divorce lawyer? He's an expert in prenups. He's a friend of Aerin's older brother. He drew up a prenup for Delphine, given her assets are worth so much more than Miguel's. In fact, it was Miguel who insisted on it, so that proves how much he loves her.'

'Does it?'

'Maybe I shouldn't have bothered bringing supper up to you.'

He heard her pick up the tray again. 'I'm sorry, Ruby.' He let out a long sigh. 'When you knocked on the door just now I was convinced a journalist had hunted me down. There were so many times in the past when the press followed me, looking for an exclusive on my parents' relationship. I hated the attention, the intrusion, the exposure. The thought of that happening again under my current circumstances—well, you can probably imagine how it feels to be cornered and unable to escape.'

Ruby put the tray back down on the table.

'I made sure no one could get to this part of the castle. I locked all the doors on my way up. Besides, I thought you might be hungry by now.'

'I am,' he said, taking her by the upper arms and drawing her closer. 'I shouldn't have kept you awake so long last night. You must be tired.'

She wound her arms around his neck. 'I can handle it.'

Lucas pressed a lingering kiss to her mouth, feeling his pulse racing at the softness of her lips, the silken touch of her tongue against his. The alluring curves of her body pressed closer and closer until he was fit to burst. He finally dragged his mouth away and placed his hands on her hips. 'So, what have you brought me to eat? It smells delicious.'

'Lots of things.' She slipped out of his hold and began serving the food onto two plates. 'I thought we could have a champagne supper up here.'

He heard the sound of bubbles being poured into glasses, and then Ruby pressed a champagne flute into his hand. The glass was cold against his fingers, and the soft hiss of rising bubbles was loud in the silence.

'What are we celebrating?' He tried but failed to keep the cynicism out of his tone. 'Another wedding at Rothwell Park that has a higher than average chance of failing?'

Ruby let out a weary-sounding sigh. 'Look, I know this wedding is triggering for you. But if you could see how much Delphine and Miguel love each other you'd know how well-suited they are.'

Lucas took a long draught of champagne before putting the glass down on the desk. 'Yes, well, that's the point, isn't it? I *can't* freaking see.' He raked a hand through his hair. 'I can't see a damn thing—and I want to so badly.'

The fear that he might never see again gripped him by the guts with a cruel hand. He knew plenty of people lived with blindness—lived good and productive lives—but he needed his sight to work at the job he loved. He could not do it without his sight.

'Oh, Lucas…' Ruby put her own glass down and wrapped her arms around his waist, her cheek pressed to his chest. 'I wish I could wave a magic wand and make everything right for you.'

Lucas absently stroked the back of her head, his emotions sawing at his insides like savage teeth. 'I don't believe in magic.

I don't believe in miracles.' His voice came out through gritted teeth.

I don't believe in love.

And yet…and yet…something was picking at the lock on his heart, trying to prise it open when all he wanted was to keep it shut.

He had been honest with Ruby over his struggle to accept permanent disability. Even more honest than he had been with his specialist. The solid, impenetrable armour he hid behind was falling off, shield by shield, plate by plate, bolt by bolt, and if he didn't do something, and do it quickly, he would be completely exposed and vulnerable.

'But I *do* believe in magic and miracles, and maybe that's enough,' Ruby said.

'It's not enough,' Lucas said, and put her from him.

He needed distance. He needed to control this relentless drive to bring her closer and let her in.

He *had* to control it.

He picked up his champagne glass and drained it, putting it down again with a thud. 'You should go back downstairs, Ruby. I'm not in the partying mood.'

The sound of music and high-spirited

revelry downstairs wasn't helping his state of mind. Three times he had heard such sounds at a wedding in his home and what had come of it? Nothing but bitterness and smashed hopes, leaving echoes of sadness in every nook and cranny of the castle.

Ruby came up behind him and placed her hand on the small of his back. A bolt of electricity shot through him. 'Can we just have our supper? The wedding will be over soon.'

Lucas turned and stared down at the pale oval of her face. She was no doubt tired and hungry, and yet she had taken the time to bring him a sample of the wedding feast. Surely the least he could do was enjoy it with her.

He brushed his bent knuckles down her left cheek, his expression rueful. 'I seem to have trouble saying no to you.'

Ruby placed her hands on his chest. 'I seem to have the same problem.' Her voice was whisper-soft, her face uptilted to his. 'What are we going to do about it?'

He could feel the soft waft of her breath on his lips and desire hit him like a punch. 'This might be a good place to start,' he said, and pressed his mouth to hers.

CHAPTER TEN

SOMETIME LATER, RUBY poured the last of the champagne into their glasses and handed Lucas his. They had finally got around to having the supper she'd brought up—but not before making exquisite love on the floor of his office. And even though they were both back in their clothes her body was still humming with aftershocks, and any tiredness she'd felt before was completely gone.

Lucas took a sip from his glass and then put it to one side. 'Would you like to dance?'

Ruby looked at him in surprise. 'What? Now?'

He held out his hands to her and she placed hers in them. 'We can hear the music from up here.' He drew her into the circle of his arms and they moved in time with the romantic ballad. 'You'll have to forgive me if I crush your toes.'

'I don't think there's much chance of that.'

There was more chance of him crushing her heart. But she didn't want to think about that now.

She breathed in the familiar smell of him, the citrus and leather scent that never failed to intoxicate her senses. 'This is nice…' She swayed in his arms, tipsy on champagne and his company.

'Mmm…' His breath stirred the hair on top of her head and a shiver coursed down her spine. 'I might have to rethink my bias against weddings. This one has been better than any I've been to before.'

Ruby glanced up at him. 'How many have you been to? Apart from your parents', I mean.'

'A few, but they bored me to tears.'

'Are the couples still together?'

'Only one.'

'Oh…'

There was a beat or two of silence, broken only by the music drifting upstairs.

Lucas stopped dancing and looked down at her. 'When will you be leaving for London?'

Something in Ruby's stomach tilted

sideways. Of course. She would be leaving this bubble of happiness sooner rather than later. Lucas was selling Rothwell Park. They couldn't stay here together for ever. She was not in some fairy tale romance with him. She was in a fling and it had a timeline.

'I—I'm not sure. We have another wedding in Gloucester in a couple of weeks, but...' She didn't know how to finish the sentence without betraying her feelings for him. Without betraying her fragile hopes that he'd return them.

Lucas held her slightly aloft, his expression inscrutable. 'I've been thinking about what happens next.' His hands gave hers a light squeeze. 'Between us.'

Ruby swallowed, and her heart skipped a beat or two. 'I have to go back to London, and you're selling Rothwell Park, so...'

He drew in a long breath and let go of her hands as the same time as he released a stream of air. 'Yes, well, about the sale...'

'You've changed your mind?'

His brows snapped together and his jaw locked tight. 'No. The sale is going ahead.'

'Oh...' Her chest deflated on a sigh.

'Why are you so fixated on this place? I told you before it's a white elephant to me. A burden I want to offload as soon as I can.'

'And I've told *you* before it's the only home I ever knew as a child,' Ruby said. 'It was the first place I truly felt safe. I hate the thought of never being able to come back here.'

He moved to stand behind his desk, as if he wanted to put a barrier between them. 'I'm sure you'll be able to come back here. Jack Livingstone is planning on turning it into a boutique hotel. You might even get mate's rates if your friend Harper asks nicely. Don't they have some sort of history?'

Ruby stared at him blankly. 'Jack Livingstone? *He's* the buyer?'

'Yes. He has a chain of boutique hotels.'

'I know who he is.' She swallowed again and asked, 'Am I allowed to tell Harper, or is this news confidential?'

He gave a loose shrug of indifference. 'Do what you like. It makes no difference now. I signed the contract electronically this morning. It actually worked in my favour when Delphine brought her wedding forward. It meant I could wrap things up a little faster.'

Ruby couldn't seem to get her head

wrapped around the fact that Lucas no longer owned his family estate. And nor could she understand how cool and detached he was being about it. Surely he felt *something* about leaving his childhood home behind?

'So, when do you plan to move out?'

'I'm also going to London soon.'

'How soon?'

His expression was still difficult to read, although there was a line of tension around his mouth. 'Don't worry. We can still see each other in London.' He pulled at the cuff of his shirtsleeve, as if it was annoying him, and added, 'That is, if you're still happy to continue our arrangement?'

Something about his tone sent a chord of disquiet through her. He sounded as cool and detached as he had when discussing the sale of his ancestral home. How long did he intend their 'arrangement' to last? And why had she allowed *him* to dictate the terms? She had given up her own agency to indulge in a fling with him that she had known from the start could never go anywhere.

At least he had been honest about it from the get-go. Brutally honest. She was the one who had conjured up a fairy tale fantasy of them staying together for ever. Just like she had as a foolish teenage girl. She had imagined a future with Lucas Rothwell in which he was madly in love with her.

Ruby sent the tip of her tongue over her carpet-dry lips. 'I'm not sure what you're offering me. "Arrangement" sounds…temporary.'

'It sounds temporary because it *is* temporary,' he said in a crisp tone. 'What else did you think I would be offering?'

Ruby pressed her lips together, her chest so tight she could barely draw in a breath. 'I've wondered after these last few days together if things have changed between us. If you have changed.'

He made a rough sound at the back of his throat. 'Why would I want to change?'

'I meant in your feelings about me.'

There was a silence so thick a pin dropping would have sounded like a metal pole crashing to the floor.

Lucas let out a curt swear-word. 'You know, I'm getting a weird sense of déjà-vu. The champagne has gone to your head if you think anything has changed in that regard. You knew the rules when we started this. You can't say I didn't tell you what to expect.'

How cruel of him to remind her of her

embarrassing teenage crush. Didn't he realise how much she regretted making such
a fool of herself back then? And she would
be making an even bigger fool of herself if
she revealed her feelings now. Better to end
things with her pride intact.

'If you don't mind, I think we should end
our arrangement now. Tonight.'

'Tonight?'

Was that a hint of shock in his tone or
was she imagining it?

'Why tonight?'

'We've both achieved our goals. Delphine's wedding has gone off without a
hitch and you've sold Rothwell Park. We
can part ways now, without hard feelings.
Or, worse, catching feelings neither of us
want.'

His forehead was screwed up in a per-
plexed frown. 'Catching feelings?'

'Falling in love.'

Lucas placed his hands on the back of his
chair, his knuckles showing white beneath
his tan. But his expression was as blank
as the wall behind him. 'Okay. We end it
now.' His voice revealed even less than his
inscrutable features.

'Thank you for allowing us to hold the

wedding here. It was very generous of you not to charge a fee and—'

He held up a hand like a stop sign. 'Can we just leave it at that?' He closed his eyes and pinched the bridge of his nose. His hand fell away from his face and he let out a rough-sounding breath and glanced in her direction. 'I hate goodbyes.'

'Yes, well… I'm not too fond of them either.' She looked at the remains of their supper on his desk. 'I'd better clear this away before I—'

'Leave it.'

'But—'

'I said, leave it.' His tone brooked no resistance.

Ruby stepped away from the desk, her heart as heavy as an anvil. 'I hope you get your sight back, Lucas.'

'Thank you.'

She hesitated by the door, wishing and hoping he would call her back and say he had made a terrible mistake. That he did love her. That he didn't want her to leave.

A sob rose in her throat at the thought of never seeing him again, but she quickly disguised it as a cough. 'Excuse me. It's been a long day. And I think all those flowers downstairs are triggering my asthma.'

'Ruby?'

She turned to look at him, glad he couldn't see the tears tracking down her cheeks. 'Yes?' She was proud of how indifferent she sounded—as if her heart *wasn't* breaking into a thousand and one pieces.

His throat rose and fell over a tight swallow. 'Thank you for helping me get through a rough time. I'm not sure what I would have done without you...especially with your gran out of action.'

'That's okay. I had a good time.'

One side of his mouth curved upwards, but it was a stretch to call it anywhere near a smile. 'Take care of yourself, won't you?'

'You too.'

There was another beat or two of silence so thick it was almost palpable. And then Ruby turned and walked out without looking back. The door shut behind her with a soft thud that sounded eerily like the closing of a book. End of story.

But this one—*her one*—didn't have a happy ending.

Lucas let out a breath and let go his iron grip of the chair and flexed his aching knuckles. He should be happy, right? The fling he shouldn't have had in the first place was over. And all done with cool politeness rather than rancour and ill feelings. Why then did he feel so...so angry? So disappointed?

A heavy weight of disappointment he could not explain was sitting in his chest. He had always intended to end his fling with Ruby. He ended all his flings with lovers. He never gave anyone the opportunity to leave him. He left first. That was one thing he had learned from his parents— the person who left had the most control, and thereby suffered the least hurt. And the one thing he avoided in life was getting hurt. Loving someone gave them the power to hurt you. Why would he allow anyone that sort of power over him? He didn't. He wouldn't. He hadn't.

And yet...

Ruby closing that door had sent a shockwave through his chest, snatching the very air from his lungs. He had intended to continue their fling a little longer. How much longer he couldn't say. It was unusual for him, but he had never had a clear idea of the timeframe on his fling with Ruby. It had been as blurry and vague as his vision...the end point had always been in the foggy distance.

But it was here. Tonight. Now. A line had been drawn through their relationship as clear as if he had drawn it himself. Ruby would leave Rothwell Park tomorrow and he would never see her again. But then he hadn't seen her for the duration of their fling. Not clearly—not in detail, not in the way he'd longed to see her.

Was that why he was so angry? Was that why he was bitter, because she had ended it so abruptly? He clenched his hands into fists, furious with himself for wanting her. For needing her. For aching for her spine-tingling touch…

He was a man who didn't need anyone. He was a man who didn't get close.

He was still that man. He hadn't changed.

He was a man who didn't love.

Ruby ran into her friends on the way back to her room. The last thing she wanted was a post-mortem on her relationship with Lucas, but Harper and Aerin were too observant to miss her reddened eyes. They followed her into her room and closed the door behind them.

'What's happened?' Aerin asked, grasping Ruby by the hand. 'Have you been crying?'

Ruby brushed at her eyes with the back of

her hand. 'I've ended things with Lucas…' She bit down on her lower lip to stop it from trembling.

'Oh, Ruby…' Harper sighed. 'Maybe it's for the best, hon. Us Cinderella-types don't belong in a rich man's world.'

Aerin handed Ruby a tissue. 'I'm so sorry. I wish there was something I could do to make you feel better.'

Ruby blew her nose. 'I'll be fine. I knew the risks when I got involved with him. He told me from the outset our fling was only temporary. But how can you put a time-frame on your feelings? How do you switch them off like that?' She snapped her fingers for effect. 'I think I've always loved him.' She choked back another sob and wiped at her eyes. 'I'm leaving in the morning. First thing. I don't want to see Lucas again.'

'Are you sure you should rush off like that?' Aerin asked with a concerned frown. 'What if he changes his mind? He might see things differently in the morning.'

Ruby's shoulders slumped on a sigh. 'He won't see things differently. He's made up his mind to live his life without needing anyone. And now I've ended the fling, be-cause to continue it knowing he's never going to change would end up hurting me more in the end.'

'Oh, I'm so sorry things have turned out like this,' Aerin said. 'But I guess you know him better than anyone else.'

'I only know what he allows me to know,' Ruby said. 'He won't let me in. I thought he was starting to—telling me stuff about his parents and so on—but when push came to shove, no. He locked me out. He refuses to love anyone. Why did I think he might love me?'

Harper eyed her for a long moment. 'Did you tell him you loved him?'

Ruby shook her head. 'No, and that's one thing I'm immensely grateful for. I couldn't bear it if I'd gushed over him like I did when I was sixteen. Urgh! Can you imagine how embarrassing that would have been?'

Harper's expression communicated her staunch approval. 'You gotta maintain your pride, sister.'

'There's something else I need to tell you…' Ruby began to shred the tissue with her fingers.

Harper looked at her in horror. 'You're not…*pregnant*?'

Her friend had a mortal fear of getting pregnant, as her own mother had done, by a man who didn't stand by her and refused to acknowledge or even meet his child because he was already married with a family. Harper had ended up in care from the age of eight, after her mother died by suicide. Although her father had promised to visit a few times after her mother's death, he hadn't followed through. And, unlike Ruby, Harper had never been chosen to live with a relative or reside with a permanent foster family.

'Of course not,' Ruby said. 'It's about the new owner of Rothwell Park.'

Harper's eyes rounded even further. 'Lucas is selling?'

'It's a done deal,' Ruby said. 'And you'll never guess who's bought it.'

The colour drained from Harper's face and she gave a convulsive gulp. 'Jack Livingstone?'

'Yep. He's going to turn it into one of his boutique hotels.'

'Well, I can safely say *I* won't ever be staying here again,' Harper said with emphatic determination.

'Nor will I,' Ruby said, with a sigh of sadness that was bone-deep.

Lucas heard Ruby's car leave before dawn the next day. He had lain awake most of the night at war with himself. One part of him had wanted to go to her, to tell her to stay, the other had wanted to push her away. It had been like revisiting the pain of his childhood, reliving the walking out of one or other of his parents and having to deal with the devastation of the other.

Watching the rollercoaster of emotions in the person left behind had left an indelible mark on him. He would not be like his mother, clawing at his father, begging him to stay, to give her one more chance. And he would not be like his father, who'd told his wife he loved her and then gone off and had affairs with younger women when his wife's up-and-down moods wore him down.

Lucas knew he was doing the right thing for himself, let alone Ruby, by letting her go. He didn't have the emotional hardware to maintain a long-term relationship. He wasn't cut out to be the fairy tale knight who rode off into the sunset with his princess. It wasn't fair to promise things he had no ability to give. It was better to let her go so she could find someone who *could* give her those things: love, commitment, a family.

But...

He would miss Ruby. Deeply. He would miss her in so many ways—the sound of her pottering about the castle kitchen, the fresh flowery scent of her fragrance, the tinkling of her laugh, the warm press of her body against his. Oh, how he would miss the sweet curves of her body. The taste and feel of her, the intensity of her kiss and her touch.

A crippling ache seized his body with a pain so violent it took his breath away. Making love with her had been the most erotic, pleasurable and exciting experience—one he would never forget. Every moment was etched on his mind, on his body, on his senses.

Lucas was glad he was moving out of Rothwell Park. Staying here now would be too hard without Ruby. She brought life to the place, she lit up the dark corners, and she added colour to every room. Not a colour he could see, but one he could sense. She brought a lightening of the sombre atmosphere…a freshness that was like a summer breeze, blowing out the stale air of sadness that had clung to Rothwell Park for so long.

He was almost glad he couldn't see Ruby drive away. He had watched his parents take turns leaving and each time it had been emotional torture, knowing he would have to pick up the pieces left behind.

But this time there was only himself to deal with, only his own emotions to handle. He still didn't get why he was so angry. So bitterly disappointed that Ruby had ended their arrangement before he was ready.

Why hadn't he been ready?

CHAPTER ELEVEN

One month later...

RUBY WAS GLAD when a rush of wedding bookings came in soon after she got back to London. Although the meticulous planning and organising of menus that involved didn't entirely take her mind off Lucas, at least it distracted her.

But being around loved-up couples who were excitedly planning their upcoming weddings was a form of torture. Why couldn't she be like them? Blissfully happy with the love of her life? If anything, she loved Lucas more than ever. How could that be? Was something wrong with her? She was supposed to be moving on with her life. A month had passed and yet she was still heartsore and lonely—*more* heartsore and *more* lonely than she had ever been. It was like being handed a grand prize and then realising it didn't belong to you after all.

Lucas didn't belong to her. He didn't belong to anyone. He was an island, not unlike his own Greek one. *Urgh*. Why did she remind herself of those wonderful days on his gorgeous island? It was like rubbing salt into a wide, seeping wound. Would it ever heal? Or would she always feel this aching sense of loss for what might have been if only things had been different?

But how could things be different if Lucas couldn't allow himself to love her? To love anyone? Or was it because she was unlovable? The old self-doubts plagued her—what if it was *her* that was the problem? Harper was right—they were all Cinderella-types who didn't belong in a rich man's world. Lucas's world had always been out of reach for Ruby. She had lived in it in a vicarious sense, on the fringe, but she had never truly belonged?

Love was supposed to conquer all, to bridge all gaps and chasms, but what hope did she have that Lucas could ever love her?

None. Zilch. *Nada*.

It reminded her of her childhood, of her gnawing relentless emotional hunger to be loved by her mother. But her mother, like

Lucas, has been incapable of it. Some people locked away their hearts or were damaged so much that they shut down their emotions.

She would never know why her mother had never loved her, but she had to assure herself it wasn't because of her—it was her mother's issue.

And she had to accept that Lucas not loving her was not because *she* was unlovable. Her gran loved her, her friends loved her— even her clients loved her.

Harper came into Ruby's office with her camera bag slung over her shoulder. 'How are you doing?'

Ruby painted a smile on her face. 'I'm fine. Distracting myself with work. You know the drill.'

'Yeah…' Harper leaned down to put her bag on the floor and winced. 'I certainly do.'

'Are you okay?'

Harper straightened and rubbed a hand at the base of her spine. 'I've got a nagging backache. I think lugging all that gear around is wrecking my spine.'

'I have some paracetamol in my handbag.'

Harper sat gingerly in one of the client's

chairs in Ruby's office. 'I've already taken some and it did nothing.'

'Maybe you should see a doctor? Or a physiotherapist?'

Harper shifted in her chair, obviously trying but failing to get comfortable. 'Nah, I'll be okay in a day or two. I probably need to lose a bit of weight and get a bit fitter—especially before I head to Paris in six weeks for the book shoot.'

Harper wasn't one to crow about her achievements, but she had been selected to contribute to a coffee table book featuring the work of up-and-coming photographers.

She focussed her gaze on Ruby. 'Speaking of weight, you look like you've lost a lot, and you've got dark circles under your eyes.'

Ruby sighed. 'Yes, well... I don't seem to have much appetite for anything just now. And I find it so hard to sleep.'

'You miss him, huh?'

'Like you wouldn't believe.'

'Has he contacted you?'

'No.'

Harper shifted her head from side to side. 'You have to move on, hon. You can't let the end of one little fling get you down.'

'I know, but I keep hoping I got it wrong

about him…that he does love me after all.'
Ruby gave a self-deprecating grimace and
added, 'Remind me how many years I did
that with my mother?'

Harper rolled her eyes. 'You and me
both.'

Lucas woke from yet another fitful sleep
and opened his eyes. Something was different… The once vague outlines of his
bedroom furniture had sharpened—not by
much, but they were less blurry and amor-
phous.

He sat upright and rubbed at his eyes,
squinting against the bright sunlight beam-
ing through the windows of his London
apartment. He threw off the bedcovers and
padded over to the window. Even from his
penthouse height, he could see more than
he'd been able to see the day before. The
stunning view should have lightened his
spirits, but if anything it did the opposite.

What was a stunning view if you had no
one to share it with?

He turned back to the bed and felt his
chest tighten at the stark emptiness of his
crumpled white sheets. He pictured Ruby in
his bed and an ache gripped him deep in his
gut. Maybe he shouldn't have come to Lon-

don. Maybe he should have gone back to his island. But going back there without Ruby would be too…difficult. And the thought of taking anyone else was unthinkable.

Would he have to sell the island? How else could he move on? He couldn't allow himself to be haunted by memories of his time with Ruby. And it had been such a short time. When it came down to it, their fling had been one of his shortest.

Why, then, was he struggling to let her go?

Because he hadn't wanted to let her go.

The realisation was like a zig-zagging bolt of lightning shooting through his brain. Of course he hadn't wanted to let her go. She had been a part of his life for years, and when the end of their fling had come he had fought against it. Fought violently. Not wanting to accept he would never see her again.

He had closed his heart to love, closed his mind to emotion, never wanting to end up like his parents. And yet he was unable to move forward because he missed Ruby so much. He ached for her in every bone of his body. He searched for her in his dreams and he woke alone and lonely in his bed, his body yearning for her. He had mistaken his feelings for simple lust, but that was a lie. A blatant lie he had told himself to protect himself from vulnerability.

The physical intimacy he'd shared with Ruby had been wonderful, but it was their emotional connection that had taken it to the next level. That was why he hadn't wanted their fling to end. He loved her with his body and his mind and his heart.

But did she love him? She hadn't said so. Was he a fool to think she would be interested in resuming their fling?

Lucas scraped a hand through his hair and sighed. He had half an hour before he was meeting his father for a quick coffee. Lionel—Lucas couldn't remember the last time he had called his father 'Dad'—was flying in for a business meeting. He could think of a dozen things he'd rather be doing this morning, but he hadn't seen his father in over a year. At least he would be able to *see* him—perhaps not as clearly as he would have liked, but still it was an improvement, and he was thankful for it.

The coffee shop was in Mayfair, and Lucas saw his father sitting at one of the tables in the window as he approached. His father was looking down at his phone, no doubt scrolling through endless emails and messages, his life so busy he could only slot in ten minutes for his son.

Lucas realised with a jolt that he was like his father in more ways than he cared to admit. Before he'd lost his sight, hadn't he been the busy man, with no time for anything but the most fleeting of relationships?

His father looked up from his phone when Lucas came to the table. 'Lucas. Nice to see you. Sit down. I've just got to send this email to my lawyer in Brazil.'

Lucas sat opposite and the waitress came over and took his order for coffee. His father continued to tap away at his phone, a frown on his forehead.

'Your lawyer?' Lucas asked when he could stand it no longer. 'Is everything all right?'

His father put his phone down on the table, his expression sheepish. 'Rosa is leaving me.'

'Should I ask why?'

'I probably deserve it.' Lionel Rothwell sighed. 'I had a tiny little fling with someone I met at a party. Rosa found out.'

'I'm starting to lose count of how many times you've been married and divorced.'

It was hard for Lucas to erase the cutting judgement in his tone. But how many times did his father have to go through this before something changed? Before *he* changed?

'I guess I'm not the settling down type...' Lionel toyed with his teaspoon. 'A little like you, I guess. Once a playboy, always a playboy, right?'

'People can change,' Lucas said. 'You can change if you're motivated enough. Do you love Rosa?'

'Of course.'

'Have you told her?'

'Heaps of times.'

'Have you shown it? Words are cheap. Actions are more important.'

But who was he to be giving his father advice on love? He hardly qualified as a relationships expert. He was a failure at relationships. He had failed at the one relationship he valued the most—his relationship with Ruby. Why hadn't he realised until this morning that his anger over her ending their fling was because he loved her?

He loved her. He loved her. He loved her.

The words were like beams of golden bright light shining into a room after a lifetime of shadows. They were like seeing sharp detail after months of seeing nothing but blurred edges. The scales had finally fallen from his eyes and he could see what had been staring him in the face all this time—he loved Ruby.

And didn't her actions tell him she felt the same about him, even though she hadn't said the actual words? He had been so locked down emotionally, so blind emotionally, he hadn't even recognised his own feelings—let alone hers.

Ruby had told him once that the thing people tried so hard to avoid was often the very thing they most needed to grow as a person. He had been avoiding love all his life. Avoiding it, blocking it, sabotaging it just like his father.

But no longer.

He was not going to run away from the fear of loving someone fully. He was not going to shy away from a wholehearted commitment. Ruby deserved her fairy tale, and he would knock himself into shape as Prince Charming if it was the last thing he did.

Lionel picked up his coffee cup, his expression mocking. 'Listen to you. What's made you such an expert on love, eh? Or should I say who?'

'Did you ever truly love Mum?'

Lionel reared back as if insulted by the

question. 'Of course.' He frowned and added, 'I married her three times, didn't I?'

'And divorced her three times.'

'Yes, well… That's all in the past.'

'But it's not,' Lucas said. 'You're reliving it now by divorcing Rosa. What about getting some counselling? Or having a go at making your relationship work instead of calling time on it or having an affair with someone else who catches your eye?'

Lionel shrugged and picked up his phone again. 'When a relationship is over, it's over.'

'I don't believe that,' Lucas said. 'I used to, but not now. You keep sabotaging your relationships because you're frightened of loving someone totally. You always have a get-out plan.'

'What's got into you?'

Lucas pushed back his chair and stood. 'I'm sorry. I can't stay. I have to see someone. Urgently. I hope you work things out with Rosa. For her sake as well as yours and the children's. Please send them my regards.'

Lionel looked at him with a frown. 'But I've come all this way to catch up with you.'

His tone sounded like a petulant child's, and it made Lucas realise again how immature his father was. His father had never truly grown up, taken responsibility or faced reality. Lucas could not bear to turn out like him. That would indeed be his biggest failure if he did. His father walked away when things got difficult. He didn't stay and work through problems, and he didn't for a moment even consider himself a part of the problem—which was a problem in itself.

Lucas gave a bark of a laugh. 'A ten-minute slot in your busy day? That's not a catch-up—that's an insult. It doesn't surprise me that Rosa's fed up if you slot her in like you do everyone else. If you love someone, you make time for them.'

Lionel had the grace to look a little ashamed. 'I'm not good at relationships... you of all people should know that.'

'I do know it—but I also know you can change if you want to badly enough.' Lucas moved around to his father's side of the table and laid his hand on his shoulder. 'Don't waste yet another opportunity for growth.'

Lionel briefly laid his hand over Lucas's. 'It was good to see you, son.'

'It was great to see you too, Dad,' Lucas said, and he meant it in more ways than one.

Ruby was in her home office, designing a menu for a wedding for an older couple who had once been childhood sweethearts but ended up marrying other people. Now in their fifties, and both widowed, they had re-connected and fallen in love all over again.

Such happy stories were part of the joy of Ruby's career, but the downside was that it made her ache for her own happy ending. Surely she wouldn't have to wait until her fifties to hear those special words from the love of her life?

She had heard nothing from Lucas—which, prior to their fling, would not have been unusual. Months, even years could go by with zero contact. But in that short time during their fling they had shared so much together—more than she had shared with anyone else. Their intimacy had made her hope he had fallen for her as hard as she had for him.

She'd tried to douse her hopes and move on with her life, distracting herself with work and spending time with her friends, but no amount of activity and socialising could ever fill the void of loneliness of having loved and lost the only person she wanted.

Ruby had just clicked 'save' on her lap-top when her doorbell rang. She wasn't expecting anyone. Harper and Aerin had been over the previous night for a movie and homemade pizza. Harper had still been complaining about her niggling backache, but she wouldn't see anyone about it. Ruby knew better than to nag, but it did worry her that Harper wasn't her usually hale and hearty and healthy self.

She pushed back her chair and peeped through the security hole in her front door. Lucas was standing there, with a bunch of red roses in one hand, and her heart came to a juddering halt. She unlocked the door and opened it, her stomach a hive of activity. Excitement, nerves, confusion, hope—all were churning around in there.

'Lucas?'

'May I come in?'

'Sure.' She closed the door once he was inside. 'I didn't expect to see you.'

Lucas handed her the roses. 'These are for you.'

His voice was so husky it sounded as if he had swallowed some of the roses' thorns.

She bent her head to smell the blood-red blooms. Trust a landscape architect to give you the real thing, not those hothouse ones without any scent.

She looked up at him again. 'You're not wearing your sunglasses.'

He smiled, and her heart gave a soft little flutter.

'That's because I can see a little better.'

'Really? I'm so thrilled for you.'

Ruby put the roses to one side, too nervous to find a vase. Did she even have a vase? She'd broken her only one a few months ago and hadn't got around to replacing it. Why was he here? Just to tell her he had his sight back? Or dared she hope he had come for some other reason?

'Ruby.' He held out his hands to her. 'Come here.'

She slipped her hands into his broad ones and it was like coming home. His fingers wrapped around hers and firmly squeezed, as if he never wanted to let her go. She had never seen his expression so tender. Had he changed his mind? Did he want to resume their fling? But how could she settle for a fling when she wanted the for ever fairy tale?

'Can you forgive me for taking this long to realise what I should have seen a month ago?' He swallowed, and then continued in the same hoarse tone. 'I love you, my darling. I think I fell in love with you the first time we kissed. I'm so ashamed it's taken me this long to understand how I feel. To even recognise how I feel.'

'Oh, Lucas…' Ruby flung herself at him so violently he almost lost his footing. His arms wrapped around her and held her tight, and it was just as well, for right then her heart was threatening to beat its way out of her chest in excitement and joy. 'I'd given up hope that you could ever feel anything for me. I can't believe you love me.'

Lucas tipped up her face so he could lock his gaze with hers. 'Does that mean you love me too? I took a gamble, hoping you do. You didn't say anything back at Rothwell Park the night of the wedding.'

'Of course I love you.' Ruby beamed up at him, so happy to be able to say it out loud at last. 'I wanted to tell you then, but my pride got in the way.'

He cradled her face in his hands, his touch so gentle it melted her heart. 'I think it was better that you didn't. I needed to suffer a bit. More than a bit, to be honest. I'm not used to feeling so wrecked after a break-up. I'm usually the one who ends a relationship. So I put it down to a bad case of pique. I only realised today that it's because I love you and want to spend the rest of my life with you.'

Ruby looked at him with wide eyes. 'Are you proposing?'

He gave a sheepish grin. 'I guess I am... But not doing such a great job of it.' He got down on one knee, holding her hands in his and looking up at her with an abundance of love. 'Will you do me the honour of becoming my wife, my life partner, my soulmate, my everything?'

Ruby hauled him to his feet and threw her arms around him again. 'Yes! How could I not want to marry you? You are the only man I could ever love. I think I've been in love with you since I was sixteen. I can't tell you how miserable I've been. There is no worse industry to work in than the weddings one when you're nursing a broken heart.'

'Oh, my poor, sweet darling.' Lucas hugged her again, resting his chin on the top of her head. 'I was miserable too. I couldn't sleep. I couldn't think straight. I was lonely, and aching for you the whole time, but I kept telling myself it was because you had ended our relationship, not me. I can't believe I've wasted the last month thinking I didn't feel anything serious about you.'

She looked up at him again. 'You said you only realised today?'

'I met my father this morning,' Lucas said with a grimace. 'It was like looking at myself in the future. He never made time for my mother, and nor does he for his present wife—who is about to become his ex-wife if he doesn't take on board what I told him.'

'What did you tell him?'

'I told him that words are empty, that actions speak louder. That he can change if he wants to badly enough.' He smiled crookedly and continued, 'And then I realised what I was saying to him applied to me… that I was at risk of turning into him in the future. A too-busy man who goes from one broken relationship to the next. You see, constant busyness was my way of distracting myself from wanting the things I told myself I didn't want. Love, commitment, a family. It wasn't until I lost my sight that I had to stop and take stock. And I hated every second of it. That's why I was such a brooding bear that day you came to the library at Rothwell Park and asked me about Delphine's wedding. I could no longer hide behind my overpacked diary and my big moneymaking projects all over the globe.

I was stripped down to my most basic, and it scared the freaking hell out of me.'

Ruby stroked his lean jaw and smiled up at him. 'I kind of like you stripped down to your most basic.'

He grinned wolfishly at her. 'We'll get to that in a minute. But first let me tell you how wonderful it is to see you. You're still a little blurry, but I can see the sparkle in your beautiful eyes. I can even see the new freckles on your cute nose.'

He lowered his mouth to hers in a kiss that spoke of deep, abiding love. A love that she could trust, that she could depend on, that she could rely on no matter what.

Lucas lifted his mouth from hers and smiled down at her with his eyes shining. 'I really should have called in on your gran to ask her permission for your hand in marriage. What do you think she's going to say about us getting married?'

'She'll probably have a heart attack,' Ruby said. 'I didn't even tell her about our fling. I wanted to, but I couldn't bear the lecture I'm sure she would have given me.'

'She'll be happy for us,' Lucas said. 'She'll be happy you've found the love of your life and happy I have too.'

'Is that how you really see me? As the love of your life?'

'I didn't think it was possible to be this happy. I was always terrified of getting too close to anyone in case they left. I think it's something I learned from my parents. Watching the repeated train wrecks of their relationship made me shy of getting into an intimate relationship where I had little or no control.' He stroked her bottom lip with his thumb. 'But you, my beautiful girl, changed everything. You brought light to my darkness. You unpicked the lock on my heart. You gave me the motivation to change and I can't thank you enough for that. Remember when you said that often the thing people try to avoid is the very thing they need to face to grow as a person? I realised I needed to stop shying away from loving someone. And that someone, I am thrilled to say, is you.'

Ruby gazed up at him with love and adoration. 'I love you with all my heart. I can't wait to be your wife. I still can't quite believe this is happening. It's like a miracle.'

'I said once to you that I didn't believe in magic or miracles, but you are both to me. You've shown me what it's like to feel whole. To embrace emotion instead of hiding from it or pretending it's something else.'

'I was so frightened I would spend the rest of my life without you,' Ruby said. 'I was trying hard to move on, but I couldn't. It was impossible to think of a future without you in it.'

'We'll have a great future because we've both learned from the past. Not everyone does. Let's promise each other we'll work through stuff together, never give up on each other.'

'I promise with all my heart.'

Lucas brought his mouth back down close to hers. 'I love you and I will always be there for you.'

And he sealed his promise with a kiss that left her in no doubt of his heartfelt commitment.

* * * * *